"COME ON!" DONAVAN YELLED DESPERATELY.

The bay surged forward and began to pick its way up the sloping wall of the hogback. A backward glance by Donavan showed the Apache scouts pulling up and holding fire as they watched the deadly bolts of lightning slam into the elevation.

Halfway up the hogback it suddenly occurred to Donavan why the Apache were holding their fire. Spilling out of the saddle, he murmured, "What attracts this lightning . . . unless . . . unless this formation is laden with iron ore!"

Then everything seemed to explode around him. He could smell seared flesh as the bay went down. For a brief moment he felt as if his entire body was being consumed by fire. Then he crumbled to the ground and felt no more. . . .

ROBERT KAMMEN
THE
WIDOW MAKERS

ZEBRA BOOKS
KENSINGTON PUBLISHING CORP.

Dedicated with much love to
Rosella Jennings,
our Mother and friend.

ZEBRA BOOKS

are published by

Kensington Publishing Corp.
475 Park Avenue South
New York, NY 10016

Second printing: April, *1990*

Printed in the United States of America

Chapter One

On the second night of Lieutenant Chase Donavan's captivity, an orb weaver began spinning its web between the bars in the only window. This was the first thing Lieutenant Donavan noticed when the morning sunlight dropped hotly upon his face. He squinted away from the glaring intrusion as somewhere in the cell compound at Fort Randall a door clanged open, followed by the measured tread of boots on concrete. A tin cup and plate were slid through the slot in the lower portion of the door. Then the footsteps passed on to halt at another cell before continuing toward the outer door. Another three days passed, with the orb weaver keeping Chase Donavan company, but when the lieutenant of cavalry slept each night, the spider replaced its old web with a new one, spun in complete darkness by touch alone.

"Another man has spun a web of deceit," said Chase Donavan to himself one lonely afternoon.

A month ago, though it seemed much longer, Chase Donavan had been just another soldier taking part in the spring campaign against the Comanche and Tonto Apache. And the new silver bar he wore had come after four lonely years out here on the Llano Estacado.

Southward a few miles lay the Pecos River; opposite there was Guadalupe Peak hinging on to the Sacramento Mountains in New Mexico. There were other tributaries snaking across the vast plains of western Texas along with the main line of the Texas and Pacific Railroad. Towns were a scarce commodity in this land claimed by both the rancher and Indian. Somehow Donavan, a man edging toward his twenty-sixth birthday, had survived—but not without paying a price, the long scar marking his left arm, compliments of a Comanche war lance, and the puckering mark of an old bullet wound at his right hip. The years spent in the saddle had hardened Chase Donavan's mind and wiry frame, with the constant wind and burning sun etching the bronzed skin tightly to the bony contours of his face. The sandy hair had thinned some, the wary blue eyes having seen death and wanton cruelty. Inwardly there was a deeper change, for Chase Donavan, though an easygoing man, seldom extended the welcoming hand to new arrivals at Fort Randall, simply because most of his old comrades in arms had been killed in these endless forays against the Indians.

So for Lieutenant Chase Donavan the sands of time were running out. Despite his wounds, he'd been lucky. Back a couple of years he had received a commendation for exemplary bravery; but ever since then, the Comanche had taken note of the tall and fair-haired officer, and Chase Donavan knew that he'd become a marked man.

Only it wasn't the Comanche who had brought about Lieutenant Chase Donavan's downfall. Two days out of Fort Randall the Coyotero Apaches working for the army as trackers came riding hard out of an arroyo and back to the main column of horsemen commanded by Major James Ramsey. The major's tight-lipped voice cut through the sultry afternoon heat.

"Column . . . halt!"

Yesterday Company H, commanded by Major Ramsey, had cut away from the regiment with orders to look for any Indian sign south of the Pecos River before circling back and rendezvousing at Rincon Wells. This had all changed, pondered Lieutenant Chase Donavan, as he listened to the guttural voice of an Apache scout named Tomas narrate to the major what they'd stumbled across.

"A dozen or so Comanche you say?" Ramsey's eyes slid to those of his lieutenant. "Well, Chase, what do you make of it?"

"Our orders, sir, didn't include engaging the enemy."

"Dammit, Lieutenant, I'm commanding here."

As Major Ramsey turned his attention to the Apache, Chase Donavan knew that it had been bad luck the major taking over Company H. Somehow staff duty back at the Pentagon had gotten too tame for James Ramsey, so he'd wrangled an assignment out here. In two months Ramsey had managed to destroy the morale of the men he commanded along with convincing Chase Donavan the man was totally unfit for frontier duty.

"Lo'tenant, I don't like what I'm overhearing," grumbled First Sergeant Matt Riddell. "Ramsey can't be serious about disobeying the colonel's orders. . . ."

Swinging his horse sideways, Donavan cast Sergeant Riddell a tired look. "Seems Ramsey's a glory seeker. Ramsey damn well knows the Commanche have been gathering their tribes together. So if some have been sighted . . . well by now they'll have ridden back to warn the main party."

"Maybe they was just some out hunting for game?"

"Let's hope so."

"Donavan, Sergeant Riddell," called out the major, "it seems we're going to have some action at last." The

7

brown eyes of James Ramsey sparkled with anticipation. He was a suavely handsome man with an erect carriage and a handlebar mustache cutting a wide swath above his square jaw. Unlike Chase Donavan, he still carried his cavalry sword, and the red sash tied to it started to flutter some as the wind began to pick up.

Both men spurred ahead and drew up by Major Ramsey, with Chase Donavan flicking a questioning glance at the Apache scout. Said Lieutenant Donavan, "I caught most of what Tomas told you, sir, that he spotted a small bunch of Comanche."

"A mile or two west of that arroyo heading southwesterly away from the river. And camped in a shallow draw. A dozen or so," Ramsey replied.

"Colonel Anderson will be pleased, sir."

"I figure he'll be even more pleased if we take action against them."

"Those weren't our orders—"

"Damn your impertinence, Lieutenant! I command here. Donavan, it seems you've been a thorn in my side ever since I took over the company. As of this moment I'll brook no more intolerance from you. We'll split our forces. You, Donavan, will take half the company and proceed westward along the riverbank. Sergeant Riddell and the scouts will go with me. We should find them around sundown. But wait for my signal before attacking. That's it, Lieutenant Donavan, gather your men and move out."

After a while when the sun began lowering, it sent blinding heatwaves dancing across the barren wastes along the river and into the eyes of Chase Donavan and the men strung out behind him. They held their horses at a canter and had stopped to let them breathe at half-hour intervals. For water they'd veer down and let the horses slake their thirst from the brackish waters of the Pecos. Chase Donavan was worried, for not only were they riding blindly into glaring sunlight, but hammering at him ever since Major Ramsey had issued his insane orders was a grim premonition that they were also riding into a trap. With the back of a gloved hand Donavan wiped the sweat from his forehead before settling the old dusty campaign hat back on his head and cursing.

"You say something, Lo'tenant?"

"Listen up!" Chase Donavan yelled. Fishing out a cigarillo, he lit it as the troopers spread along the river moved his way. "It can't be more than a mile to where we come to that draw. There'll be no talking from here on in. Make sure your weapons are ready . . . and if you spot anything—meaning a Comanche or even Apaches . . . don't be bashful about telling me."

"Sir," spoke up a corporal, "it seemed our orders was to avoid a fight if at all possible."

"It seems the commanding officer of Company H wants to fight his own war—no matter who gets killed. Mount up!"

As he rode, Lieutenant Chase Donavan couldn't help thinking that he was getting old. Maybe too old for this kind of work. Though there was still in Chase Donavan a love for soldiering, and he was good at it, it seemed that didn't matter now, nor would any of his hard-gained experience help them if they ran into the main body of Commanche. By rights he should leave Major Ramsey to his own uncertain fate simply by cutting southward toward Rincon Wells. But he owed it to the men with Ramsey. Pulling up on the crest of a timbered break, Donavan could feel the presence of his men to either side as his squinting eyes tried to pierce the blinding sunlight from under the brim of his shading hat.

"They're close," he finally said, along with giving the command to unsheath their rifles.

"Too damned close!" someone called out, as sporadic gunfire came from the south.

"Steady now!" Chase Donavan told his men.

"What do you make of it, Lo'tenant?"

"I figure the major's found that war he was looking for . . . the damned fool." Chase Donavan's upraised arm caused his men to rein up. "There's some Indians up on that arroyo wall. From here it looks as if they've got Major Ramsey boxed in."

"And more of them Comanche pouring in from the west."

"Might as well go earn our pay," Donavan said grimly. He surveyed the long stretch of high ground they were on, and the few screening mesquite and scrub oak. Some distance ahead the ridge dipped sharply, then rose again to form part of the arroyo the Comanche were occupying. His decision made, Chase Donavan barked, "We'll hit those coming in out of the sun, those to the west. With any luck we should hook up with Ramsey's men . . . or even chase the Comanche away." Another arm signal brought Donavan and his troopers forward.

They came riding hard down from the elevation, spreading out more as they picked out individual Comanche. Leaden slugs from their carbines cut into the flesh of Indian or horse, and the charge of the Comanche faltered. Chase Donavan found himself at the left flank of his command, as most of his men surged down toward the bottom of the arroyo. To Donavan's surprise there appeared a couple of cavalrymen, with one of them, it seemed, trying to keep another from fleeing the scene of the ambush. As Chase reined up hard, Major James Ramsey twisted in the saddle and fired back at Sergeant Matt Riddell, and then to Chase's disbelieving eyes, the major fired again, causing the sergeant to spill out of his saddle. Suddenly

10

Major Ramsey became aware of Donavan riding in, and he swiveled his handgun to cover the lieutenant.

"Dammit, Ramsey, that was cold-blooded murder!"

"You won't live to tell about it!"

"You cowardly bastard . . . you were running away. . . ." He could see the crazed and twisted set to the major's face, and carefully Chase Donavan raised the arm holding his own service revolver so that the barrel pointed skyward. "Easy, Ramsey, there's no place to go . . . but back to your troops."

As some sense of sanity returned to Major James Ramsey, with it came the shocking fear he'd gunned down one of his men, and the terrible consequences of what this meant. The only witness to his act of cowardice was this man, Donavan. Ramsey's finger tightened on the trigger, then lightened as he calmed down. Then it came to him, just what he was going to do, and a vicious smile lifted his mustache.

"Drop your gun!"

Donavan complied.

The major spurred in closer "You shouldn't have done it, Lieutenant. So by rights I should kill you now." He brought his horse in behind Donavan's, then reversed his hold on the revolver and struck Donavan at the back of his head, and Chase Donavan fell unconscious to the ground.

"Now," said Major Ramsey as he looked around guardedly, "you'll be courtmartialed for cowardice and murder. While I receive a commendation. Yes . . . this will work out nicely." Dismounting, he fished a short piece of rope out of a saddlebag and used it to tie Chase Donavan's wrists together. He had just lifted Donavan aboard his horse when several troopers from Company H came pounding into view.

"Sir," yelled a corporal, "them Comanche have pulled out!"

"As I knew those cowards would," responded the major. Then in response to their questioning eyes, Ramsey said, "Lieutenant Donavan killed the sergeant in cold blood. The charges will be desertion and murder. Now we'll head for Rincon Wells, gentlemen."

Once again the sun fell below the western horizon as Chase Donavan prepared to face another lonely and apprehensive night in his cell. He hadn't gotten used to being locked up, and Chase was absolutely certain that his sentence would be death by hanging. Pacing the cell, he wondered again why Major Ramsey hadn't gunned him down out there. The answer could lay in the fact the major had influential friends in both Washington and Division Headquarters in St. Louis. Cutting right to the gristle, Chase knew it would be his word against that of a superior officer's.

"Yup, my word against that of a murderer and coward."

He swung away from raindrops splattering through the barred window and slumped down on the hard cot. On the chair by the cot lay a tobacco pouch compliments of a sentry, one of those who'd been in Company H. He rolled a cigarette into shape, and smoked it while stretched out on the cot. After a while he crunched out what remained of the cigarette on the floor and tried to let sleep drive Fort Randall and what had happened to him from his despairing thoughts. Much later that same evening a key easing into the lock in his cell door jarred Chase Donavan's eyes open.

"Easy," someone whispered.

Chase dropped his legs to the floor as he sat up. As his eyes adjusted to the pale light of night he could make out the outline of an enlisted man, the large yellow stripes on either sleeve denoting the man was a corporal.

"Lieutenant, I won't tell you my name, only that I'm assigned to Company H—that I'm here to get you out of this cell."

"That so?" Chase said warily. "Maybe the major is behind this. . . ."

"Major Ramsey," the corporal whispered back, "is one reason I'm here. Now listen up, Donavan." He eased down on the chair. "I saw it all, Lieutenant Donavan . . . the major panicking and riding out . . . Sergeant Riddell going after Ramsey just to keep the bastard alive. Then your bunch showed up and drove them Comanche away. But that was all I seen, the sergeant and Major Ramsey vanishing over rimrock. Later him returning with you slung over your saddle. Now you're facing certain death . . . sir."

"You could be a witness at my courtmartial—"

"That's all changed," the corporal interrupted bitterly. "A couple of the other men who knew what happened talked too loudly about going to the post commandant. Next thing I knew they went out on patrol and got themselves killed. The same'll happen to me I go see Colonel Taylor. It boils down to, Donavan, that Major Ramsey is getting worried. I figure this means he can't afford to have you stand trial. That he'll try to have you killed before that."

"I'll take my chances."

"Sorry, Donavan, but it's all set up, your escaping tonight. You stay here, Ramsey'll do you in . . . poison your chow . . . have someone use a knife on you on some dark night. Later, maybe, you can do what you like to try and clear your name. Now I reckon it's my duty to keep you alive. That means vamoosing tonight."

Chase Donavan ran a thoughtful hand along his temple, then he fastened a rueful smile and said, "For

13

certain Ramsey's got the deck stacked against me. Trouble is, I never ran from anything in my life."

"You're sure as sin an innocent man . . . so you won't exactly be running."

"Yes, I suppose you're right, Corporal."

"Got a horse all saddled and tied outside the stockade." He eased out of she cell first, then closed the iron door when Donavan was out in the narrow corridor. From there it was merely a matter of leaving the cell block and crossing the rain-enshrouded parade ground to the main gate, where much to Donavan's surprise, another man attached to Company H was on guard duty.

Opening the gate, the sentry muttered, "Sir, best of luck to you. But you know them Apache scouts'll be after you come morning."

Nodding, and casting both the sentry and the corporal a smile, Donavan slipped out through the gate and soon found the horse along with the spare clothing and rain slicker. Donning the extra clothing, Chase led the horse at a walk to the west until he was well away from Fort Randall and all of its bitter memories.

"Now, hoss," he pondered as he mounted, "Mexico's southward. Which is where they'll figure I'm headed."

Lieutenant Chase Donavan rode on until he came to a stream. He spurred down into it and let the deep-chested bay joggle along its shallow waters in a northerly direction. Dawn found him far out on the Llano Estacado. The sky was a molten blue, a high sky with just a sprinkling of clouds hugging above the Rocky Mountains. That afternoon he crossed into New Mexico, but the land remained the same, just a wide swath of plains dotted with a few creeks and mesas. That afternoon Chase realized, though he hadn't spotted them, the Coyotero Apache scouts had picked up his trail. An ingrained sixth sense, one acquired after years of soldiering in the west, told Chase that. A less experienced man would bring his horse into a gallop and probably ride it to death, but though worry settled under his hat, he held the bay at a steady canter.

At times the stretch of plains he rode over seemed barren. But eastward a few miles lay the beginnings of such rivers as the Sulphur, White, and the North Fork of the Red River, all of them encroached upon by cowtowns. Nightfall found Chase making camp along still another, the Canadian. He was careful to keep the bay snubbed nearby to the branch of a scrub oak, and he lit no campfire to drive back night's growing chill.

"What now?" he asked the darkness.

If he did indeed manage to get away from those pursuing him, where could a man suited to army work head? There were places where gold or silver had been discovered. Farther north up in Montana there were the copper mines of Butte. Perhaps it would be better just to strike out for the Rockies and try his hand at being a mountain man. Truthfully, Chase Donavan knew he was ill-prepared for all that had happened. Long-range plans weren't included in the itinerary of a frontier soldier. You simply made your wife or mistress or folks back east beneficiaries to your insurance policy and went out to do battle with marauding Indians. Now a bitter smile etched across Chase Donavan's wide mouth, for those charges of murder and cowardice brought against him meant his insurance policy had been cancelled. Casting the past away with a tired shrug, he dropped to one knee and reached into one of the saddlebags for that last hunk of beef jerky and the piece of hardtack. When he'd propped his back against the saddle, Chase ate slowly as the night grew blacker. The absence of the moon seemed to bring roving coyotes in closer, and along with their yip-yapping came the distant wailing of a wolf. They were comforting

15

sounds, as was the distant rolling of thunder to the southwest. And the cavalry mount snorted and pawed nervously at the hard-packed ground as the man who'd brought it here fell into a restless sleep.

Long before sunup Chase Donavan was saddle-bound. He knew those tracking him had cut considerably into his lead of around a day's travel. They would be led by Tomas, a damned good tracker, one Chase called a friend. Or so he hoped. But if his hunch was right, Major James Ramsey had issued orders to kill. This was something the other Coyotero Apache scouts would relish for the sake of killing more than the bonus Ramsey surely had promised them.

Distantly he spotted a small bunch of antelope grazing out in the open as Chase's eyes swung westward to the vague peaks of the Rockies. They were still at least two days away. Could he make it that far on his tiring horse? Realizing those chasing him would have spare mounts, Chase Donavan said worriedly, "Anything will be better than dying out here on these plains."

Later that day, just past nooning with the hot sun glaring almost overhead, he jogged the bay through a parched creek bottom. Loping onto prairie again, he came upon scattered bunches of Longhorns and soon a deserted line shack. He swung the bay in and sought the little fringe of shade along the north wall. Swinging to the ground, Chase shoved open the front door and went inside. There was a potbellied stove, a table and two chairs, with the cupboard bringing him over to search through its shelves for provisions. He found an unopened can that had its label torn away. A field mouse scurried across the hard-packed dirt floor as Chase slumped down at the table and took out his pocket knife.

"*Hombre,* you're on Matador land!"

Startled, Chase Donavan stared through the open

door at two cowhands sitting their broncs. He shoved up from the chair, passed over the threshold and said, "I was just passing through."

The waddies, both men in their middle thirties, laid flinty eyes upon Chase's dusty uniform. They hadn't drawn their handguns, but in their eyes Chase could see a guarded wariness. The one who'd spoken before glanced over at the bay, then let his eyes sweep southward before looking at Chase again.

"We sighted you a couple of hours ago. Strange a cavalryman would be out thisaway on his lonesome —"

"As I said, I'm just passing through."

"And in some kind of a hurry."

He looked at the other waddy. A rueful grin tugged at Chase's lips, "My apologies for trespassing on Matador land. And helping myself to this can . . . and whatever's in it. Name's Lieutenant Chase Donavan."

"One of those stationed at Fort Randall?"

"Yup."

"Who's chasing you, Lo'tenant, the army or some Indians?"

"Some Apaches," he replied truthfully.

"How many?"

"Around half a dozen."

"I'll lay it out plain and simple, Lo'tenant. Our job is to protect Matador cattle. Not some wandering soldier. So the quicker you vamoose out of here, the better I'll like it."

"Fair enough. You wouldn't know where I could get a fresh horse?"

"Not likely."

"How far am I from the nearest settlement?"

"Too damned far."

The other waddy threw in, "Actually you're a few miles out of Texas. That hump of land northward is Black Mesa; farther along there's Mesa de Maya . . .

17

and if you get that far . . . some settlements along the Purgatoire River. But it just might be when them Apache spot us they'll give up chasing you, as there's other Matador hands working nearby." Opening one of his saddlebags, the cowhand lifted out a hunk of dried beef and tossed it at Chase. "That should tide you over."

Nightfall caught up with Chase Donavan near the lower reaches of Mesa de Maya. He rode up and found a level place. A short while ago he'd watered the bay and refilled his canteen at a nameless creek. Unsaddling his mount, he tied its reins to the branch of a small fir tree before hunkering down with the chunk of dried beef and his canteen.

Slowly the heat of day gave way to an increasing chill. Southward the moon was full, letting Chase study the way he'd just ridden. Sometime tonight, if they hadn't given up the hunt, Tomas and the rest would be on the prowl for him, for they could track by moonlight even though Chase had taken pains to hide his trail. From the mesa and eastward the sky lay thick with stars. Opposite, it seemed to Chase that clouds were drifting over the distant mountains. As it got colder, he thought about spreading out his bedroll.

"Nope," he said ruefully, "they'll be here tonight."

Between the long moments when he dozed off, Chase Donavan could feel the wind slowly picking up as more cloud cover came from the southwest to link up with those clouds closing in from the west. Now he could smell the rain, with the sullen clamor of thunder sweeping in across the moon-dusted plains. But he held to that rocky ledge while scanning the southern approaches to the mesa. At last, beyond the stubbly trees lining an errant creek bed, and a good four or five miles away, a mule deer buck and three doe bolted out of a hidden arroyo to go bounding away. Perhaps, pondered Chase, a pack of wolves had flushed out those deer. And if so, those wolves would be calling to one another.

"Tomas."

That name fled between Chase's lips as rain began striking the parched ground. Then in the sudden flare of lightning he could make out several horsemen loping out of the arroyo to spread out more as they headed for the creek. It began raining harder, the wind gusting more and picking up dust to fling it around Chase. *The rain'll cover my trail just enough to get me to them settlements along the Purgatoire River,* he thought as he made a grab for his saddle.

Garbed in the rainslicker and saddlebound, Chase Donavan urged the bay into a steady gallop once he cleared the mesa. He rode in a northwesterly direction, drawn that way by his remembrance of an army map detailing this chunk of territory. The Purgatoire could be no more than thirty miles away. But he was aboard a tired horse. When the bay stumbled coming over an elevation, Chase sawed back on the reins to bring it into a weary canter. Now there was no moonlight or stars; so he rode by the increasing glare of lightning, and pure instinct. Though the savage rainfall did away with trailing dust, the shod hoofmarks of the bay left an occasional imprint in the ground, and Chase knew it was only a matter of time before the Coyotero Apache picked up his trail and divined where Chase was heading.

Desperately he muttered, "But if it means killing you Tomas—or someone else—so be it." He framed a picture of the scout, Tomas: high sunken cheekbones and fathomless black eyes in a walnut-colored face. He thought back to the last military action he'd been involved in, when Major Ramsey had murdered one of

19

his men. Without question Chase knew that Tomas had seen Sergeant Riddell take out after the fleeing Major James Ramsey. He also knew the Apache wouldn't endanger himself by telling what he knew. Anyway, it would be the word of a lying Indian against someone from the military establishment. As for the immediate present, Tomas was just carrying out orders. Out here that meant either kill or be killed. Chase Donavan could accept that. But once he reached the settlements, Chase figured Tomas would give up the chase and return to Fort Randall. Unless, and he gritted his teeth in a scowl, the bonus promised by Major Ramsey had been too tempting, meaning enough *dinero* for Tomas to give up scouting and return to his people a rich man.

"Expect the worst," Chase told himself as he loped through some rocky ground and grunted as the bay swept down to land hard on the beginnings of the flood plain of the Purgatoire. He found himself tearing into the underbrush before managing to rein up and get his bearings. He rode on to reach the southeastern bank of the river, knowing this summery rainfall would soon flood the sluggish waters. Upon crossing he could feel the current gaining strength as its sinews of water clutched at his legs and the bay. He climbed onto the far bank and kept on the move until he gained higher ground overlooking the flood plain. Wheeling the bay around, Chase stared across the river and beyond. Now the lightning was almost continuous, searing the air and making the tired horse tremble under its rider. Someplace across the river a bolt of lightning knifed into a cottonwood; there was a brief fire put out by the torrential rainfall.

It came to Chase Donavan then, the lonely and terrifying knowledge that his pursuers were close at hand, and he cursed despairingly, "Dammit . . . what did

Ramsey promise you Apaches . . . half the gold in Texas?"

He draped his hand over the butt of his handgun when a horseman appeared where the floodplain joined with prairie land. The rider drew up warily. For a moment the sky grew black, leaving Chase in darkness, then a lightning flared to reveal four more Coyotero Apache lined along the far escarpment to the southeast.

Without hesitating, Donavan wheeled the bay around. Later he was to find out that if he'd ridden to the southwest some twenty miles by following the Purgatoire, he would have found haven at Trinidad, a waystop on the Santa Fe Trail. But it wasn't to be, for some primeval instinct caused Chase to urge his mount onto the rugged land lying northwest of the river. The immediate terrain was rugged and rock-laced, and through it he rode recklessly, letting the bay pick its own pace while he clung tiredly to the saddle. Most often the landscape was etched under the glare of lightning as the rain came down harder. Spurring around a boulder, he reined up on a rise and twisted in the saddle to scan his backtrail. Chase gritted his teeth to drive away the sudden spasm of fear when he spotted the Apache scouts strung out about a mile to the southeast. One of them brought his rifle up and fired, the reverberating roar of the Sharps rifle swept away by a roll of thunder.

"Now it's only a matter of time," Chase said quietly, and he brought the bay around and into a desperate run for shelter of some kind.

Without warning the terrain began sloping upward, and it was littered with juniper, and spiny yucca reaching out to tear at Donavan as he passed. And without warning the bay stumbled, throwing its rider out of the saddle. Somehow Chase managed to cling to the reins,

21

but the wind was driven from his lungs when he slammed onto the ground. The bay fell onto its side, and when it struggled upright, Chase noticed that it was favoring its right foreleg.

Struggling to his feet, he said anxiously, "Easy now . . . easy." He moved in closer and managed to calm the bay down while running a hand along its foreleg. "Dammit . . . you've thrown a shoe . . . but that can't be helped now. . . ."

He sought the saddle again. Only now, when he reined ahead, did Chase Donavan suddenly realize what confronted him, and he drew up instantly. His awestruck eyes lifted to a hogback, a natural formation stretching high above him. Along the capstones of the hogback there seemed to be rocks piled in untidy rows as though placed there by Indians. All at once there was something familiar about this rocky barrier, and Chase couldn't help recalling how similar it was to Hadrian's Wall in Great Britain. The massive barrier fled into the darkness on either side, leaving Chase with no other choice but to attempt a perilous climb over it, a climb that would leave him at the mercy of the seemingly continuous bolts of lightning that were striking down and into the hogback along its entire rising length. The frequent strikes brightened up the awesome structure as the air around Chase filled with a sulphuric stench and static electricity. Now a leaden slug punching into a nearby juniper made up Chase Donavan's mind even as his mount whickered in fear and tried to swing away from the hogback.

Another rifle sounded; and this time Chase felt something slam into his side, and he almost toppled out of the saddle. "Come on!" he yelled desperately. The bay surged forward and began to pick its way up the sloping wall of the hogback. A backward glance by Chase showed the Apache scouts pulling up and holding their fire as they watched, as Chase had done, the deadly bolts of lightning slamming into the elevation. Somehow they sensed no horseman could survive the certain death lancing down from the stormy sky.

The one called Tomas spoke in Apache, "I have heard of this place. It is sacred. If the gods decree it, Donavan will survive."

"And if so?"

"He has a better chance of surviving the bite of a diamondback."

Halfway up the natural formation of the hogback, it suddenly occurred to Chase that the scouts were still holding their fire. And with good reason he knew, for in his climb he'd been seared by lightning as the strikes seemed to go on unceasingly. Spilling out of the saddle, he was forced to urge the bay upward, and he murmured wonderingly, "What attracts this lightning . . . unless . . . unless this formation is laden with iron ore?" He was tiring fast because of his wound and the fear pounding away at him whenever lightning came seeking the hogback.

Then everything seemed to explode around Chase. The massive lightning strike lanced down between a nearby boulder and his mount. He could feel seared flesh as the bay went down quivering and dying, Chase cried out in agony. For a brief moment he felt as if his entire body was being consumed by fire. He crumbled down and felt no more.

A rustling noise echoed into the arousing mind of Chase Donavan. Something seemed to be tugging at his leg. Now his entire being was consumed with pain, while morning sunlight pierced away the comforting blackness and brought more agony to an opening left eye. When his vision cleared, it was to show Chase the

23

turkey vulture pecking away at his leg.

"Scat!" he yelled weakly, along with managing to raise a protesting arm. Horror at the presence of other vultures rising into the still air grimaced his mouth. It came to him then that he was still alive. But why couldn't he see out of his right eye? He remembered being shot in his side . . . the terrible lightning storm . . . Tomas and the other Apache scouts watching from below as he tried to scale the hogback.

Chase realized that he was laying spread-eagled on his back. As his vision cleared more, he could make out the dim outline of the dead horse. The iron bit of the bridle had been blown out of the bay's gaping mouth, while the driving force of the lightning had torn away the other front shoe, which lay near Chase's left hand. Pushing his upper body away from the ground, he reached out to find that the iron horseshoe had been twisted out of shape and still retained some heat.

He fought down the feeling of nausea and self-pity, somehow rejoicing in the fact he was still alive and the scouts were gone. This meant he would live. "Take stock of your hurts . . . dammit." It came to him then, had he been on the other side of the horse he would have taken the full brunt of the electrical charge, would have been killed instantly. "Luck still hasn't . . . run out. . . ."

Weakened by loss of blood, still in a state of shock, Chase struggled over and found the canteen. With fumbling hands he managed to remove the cap to drink his fill. Then he used some of the water to cleanse the wound at his side and tore a piece of shirt away to plug the small bullet hole. Only now did he lift a probing hand and explore the right half of his face where the pain seemed to be so intense, as well as along his right temple and hairline. Shaking away the awful pain, he worked his way around the horse, and it was with some effort that he pulled the carbine out of its scabbard only to find that the lightning bolt had rendered the weapon useless by twisting the barrel out of shape. But he needed a crutch, along with the iron determination to scale the upper reaches of the hogback and find his way beyond and to the settlements.

It took Chase Donavan the better part of two hours, this by taking long breathers, the pain and his weakening condition screaming at him to simply lie down and die. He went on to work his way over the narrow capstone crest, where disappointment etched itself across Chase's stoic face when he saw just more prairie land to the north and the Rockies lurking westerly. Once or twice he fell coming down off the hogback, and around the middle of the day he stumbled upon spring water gushing out of the ground and into a small pond hemmed by brush and scattered rock. At its edge he dropped to his knees and leaned heavily on the carbine as his bearded countenance gaped up at Chase from the reflecting and clear waters.

"My God!" he stammered. He found that the right half of his face had been disfigured and the flesh eaten away by lightning. His hair had been burned away to leave barren skin along the crown of his head. At that moment the pain intensified when he focused with his other eye on the damaged socket where his right eye had been.

Overcome by remorse and hatred for all that had happened, and weakened by his wounds, the unlucky Chase Donavan felt himself toppling forward into the shallow pond of chilly water. "Let me drown . . . let me drown."

He surfaced gasping for air. With the last of his strength and willpower Chase dragged his upper body out of the water, and then he let go, letting the first vestiges of blessed unconsciousness take away some of his pain and anger and hatred.

"Let me die . . ."

Sometime later as the sun began sinking beneath the distant mountains, a black-billed magpie winged down onto a nearby rock. Hopping down, it came over and began pecking at the strange intruder's outstretched arm, only to flutter away when a coyote trotted out of the shadows. The wily coyote caught the man scent and spun to lope away. Clearing the low ground near the pond, the coyote heard the downwind sound of saddle leather before glimpsing a pair of riders coming in from the west.

The man on the dun-colored horse, Hilario Madrid, said, "I'm glad we got here before nightfall, my son."

"*Si*, but I'm so hungry I could have eaten that coyote."

The elder Madrid was a patron of a Spanish settlement along the Purgatoire River. Though Hilario Madrid managed to raise a few goats and chickens, he worked on nearby ranches, as did his son and the other Mexicans. The Madrids had been allowed to go home for the weekend, but due to a late afternoon start, it had been decided by the elder Madrid to overnight at the spring beside which Donavan lay unconscious.

Hilario Madrid's bronc caught the scent of blood first and began prancing sideways and fighting the bit. "*Facil* . . . it is too late in the day for such nonsense." Now he motioned his son to rein up his horse, and with a hand on the butt of his sheathed rifle, Madrid urged his dun down toward the pond. At first in the failing light he couldn't tell what had alarmed his horse. As he pressed on to move around a juniper and settled his eyes upon the still form of Chase Donavan, Madrid slid

26

to the ground and went forward cautiously.

He used the toe of his scrubby boot to turn the inert form over, only to draw back some when he viewed what had happened to the face of the man at his feet. Kneeling, he felt for a pulse by placing a finger at the man's neck.

"*El es vivo*—but . . . pray tell . . . what brings a *soldado* to this place?"

Chapter Two

Most startling to Raven Keepseagle was the depth of her love for the man she'd married barely a month ago. That she could love at all was even more surprising. One day, years ago, a whiskey peddler had turned up at the Cherokee town of Owasso; whereupon a deal had been struck by Raven's father with the comely seventeen-year-old finding herself a common-law wife. The next half-dozen years found Raven Keepseagle traveling with the whiskey peddler from town to town in territorial Oklahoma. To this union a man child was born, Jesse Colder. But even through the pangs of childbirth the beatings and cursing from her husband went on, and after a while the new child became just as much a burden to his father as had Raven.

They'd been bound for Pawhuska to sell whiskey to the Osage when it happened, whiskey peddler Micha Colder reining up sharply and cursing around his drunkenness as he lurched down off the front seat of his wagon. Once he stumbled and fell into the side of the wagon, which only served to enrage the portly man. Then he was wrenching down the tailgate and hollering at his wife.

"You damned squaw! Get out, I tell you!" His eyes landed on the boy huddling under a thin coverlet.

Then he grabbed his son's arm and pulled him out of the wagon.

"No!" Raven Keepseagle screamed.

Yanking the revolver out of its holster, the peddler thumbed back the hammer and yelled, "Leave that rifle be, damn you! Out, I say! You damned flea-ridden squaw. I've been cursing the day I took you on." As the woman jumped down, he clubbed her alongside the head, and she went tumbling.

"There!" he snarled. "It'll be dark soon. Then maybe the wolves or some outlaws can have their sport." He dropped the barrel of his gun to cover Jesse Colder, going on five, bewildered and frightened by the strange behavior of his father.

The gun in Micha Colder's hand barked, causing a slug to pierce the leg of the cowering boy. As the boy cried out, the peddler swung the gun toward his wife, but then the horses lurched forward and he broke away.

"Damn . . . hold up now. Should have killed her too." Micha Colder managed to reach the front of his whiskey wagon, pile up into the seat and find the reins. Then he rode away, cursing drunkenly and never looking back.

When the young Cherokee woman came around, her first instinct was to help her son. At first in the darkness she didn't know the boy had been shot, only that they'd been left to die by her husband. "Jesse . . . we . . . we must find shelter." She reached out to touch Jesse's shoulder, then held her hand there upon realizing he was more than asleep. "Jesse?" What was this, blood?

Crouching by her son, Raven gazed wildly around, up and down the dusty road first, now to the deeper abyss of some trees off to her left. Tenderly she picked up Jesse Colder, her only possession, and love, and carried him under the trees and laid him down. In her past with the Cherokees, she'd seen the squaws take care of the sick and wounded, which first meant cutting off the blood flowing out of the lower leg wound. She tore a piece of dress away and wrapped it tightly above the wound. There was no time to think about what had happened as she set about gathering firewood, venturing amongst the trees through which she could see a stream a short distance away. Once she'd formed a campfire, Raven used two pieces of quartz to start a fire by striking them together, a tedious process that took her about fifteen anxious minutes. When the flames had taken hold, she added more wood before moving her son closer.

"Why would a man shoot . . . his own son—" Part of it had been because Micha Colder was drunk again, she knew, as she removed Jesse's tattered pants and gazed at the jagged bullet hole. To her dismay Raven saw that the slug had shattered the boy's right kneecap, and perhaps part of it was still lodged in there.

The boy stirred and called out in Cherokee, "Mother?" The shock of what happened still showed in his dark brown eyes.

"Jesse, I'm here. I must clean your wound. There is a nearby stream."

"Don't leave me!"

"My son . . . you must be brave." Reaching out, she placed her hand alongside his face and forced a smile. "It will only take a few minutes."

Springing to her feet, Raven Keepseagle hurried through the small copse of trees and padded down to the small stream glowing under starlight. It was a warm summery night, still retaining most of the heat of day, and since it hadn't rained for over a month, the air felt dry to the touch. But Raven was unaware of this as she knew that to cleanse her son's wound meant ripping away some more of her only apparel, the worn

30

gingham dress. Since her husband had disapproved violently of Raven's wearing the more suitable buckskin dress, often saying that it was laden with fleas, the one she had on now would have to sustain more damage, and somehow she didn't care. But she really suspected that the whiskey peddler wanted her to wear the gingham dress because it revealed more fully Raven's lissome figure. Her black hair hung down her back in braids, and her face was oval with high sunken cheekbones and had a haunting quality about it that at once spoke of Raven Keepseagle's great beauty and a certain sadness. Never had she worn makeup, or known the company of other women ever since being sold to the whiskey peddler, or known love. Raven's eyes were widely spaced, contained mystery in their purplish depths, could be bold or demure or obedient as occasion demanded, but had a certain soft-lashed beauty all their own. In their travels there had been many men who'd made bold advances, only to be threatened with bodily harm by the whiskey peddler. As for Raven, she considered herself to be too skinny and dark of skin, while the years with Micha Colder had taught her to hate and distrust white men.

After Raven had torn a sleeve of her dress away, she soaked the material in the cold water and hurried back through the trees. Since her only concern was for Jesse — nobody could be within miles of this deserted spot — the whickering of a horse when Raven reached the campfire brought her startled eyes up to a man seated in the saddle just beyond the farmost reaches of the flames. Guardedly her eyes flicked to a broken piece of branch as Raven fought down the momentary sense of panic.

"For certain you're not Osage," the stranger said after a while, during which he'd let his gaze play over Raven Keepseagle. "Well, just what happened?"

31

"My son was shot."

"At least you speak American. Easy . . . lady, I mean no harm. I passed through Osage territory today. Passed a whiskey peddler heading there . . . and now I've come upon you. Any connection?"

Her temper flaring at the stranger's intrusion into her private life, Raven snapped, "No."

"Okay, just asked. But from the looks of this campfire, you don't have any supplies . . . and that boy needs tending to bad. May I ride in?"

"I . . . I could use your help."

Riding in under the trees, the stranger swung down before unhooking his saddlebags. Then, when he strode closer to the campfire, the Cherokee woman got her first glimpse of the man who was to become her husband. She recoiled upon seeing the man's scarred and disfigured face and, when the man removed his brown Stetson and crouched by her son, the thatch of white hair streaking down the right side of his head. Eventually he stopped ministering to her son, removed his leather coat and told Raven to put it on.

"Now you'd better fetch my bedroll, ma'am. You and the boy can overnight in it. Done what I could. But his knee's tore up real bad. He'll need the services of a sawbones which means we'll strike out for Bartlesville at first light."

"You are very kind."

Around a brief smile he said, "This is an awful barren place. What do they call you?"

"I'm Raven Keepseagle. . . ."

"Cherokee," he murmured. "Mind if I swap my coat for that bedroll?"

As she removed the coat, their eyes locked in some unspoken bond, and Raven heard herself inquiring as to the stranger's name. After he told her, the stranger tended to his horse. He came back carrying his saddle

32

and placed it across the campfire from the woman and her son. Settling down with his head propped on the saddle, he sought the solitude of sleep as Raven Keepseagle, snugged in beside her son, stared at her benefactor.

"Chase Donavan," she said softly, "you are a very kind man. But, I sense, an unhappy one. Though if you hadn't come along, we might have perished out here."

Scarcely three months later Raven Keepseagle found herself staring out of a hotel window in Elk City, one of territorial Oklahoma's westernmost towns. Ever since meeting Chase Donavan things had changed for the better. She'd learned he was a roaming gambler and a lonely man in whom there seemed to be some deep sadness and pain. They had hung around Bartlesville as her son mended, though there'd been little the doctor could do about repairing the damage to Jesse Colder's knee. To her surprise the man Donavan had paid for her lodging at a boardinghouse and the medical bills. Mostly Donavan's awkward attempt at courting had taken the form of long walks just outside of town or a few buggy rides. He had spoken to her of something called the Homestead Act, had said that a lot of land would be up for grabs to those adventurous enough to risk the dangers. Soon they were married by a Baptist preacher and heading west. They arrived in Oklahoma City, which was packed with those waiting to claim new lands: farmers from back east, the unemployed, merchants, bankers and even some cowboys. But when the signal came and the federal troops stepped aside to let the great land rush begin, the man she had married watched as thousands broke away from Oklahoma City and westward.

33

Now here they were in Elk City, with Chase Donavan out buying the supplies they would need to begin a homestead. She never questioned his not going with the others, even though most of the good land in the Cherokee Outlet, other land once a part of the Tonkawa and Pawnee reservations, had by now been claimed by the horde of white men. Raven was finding out that she knew little about Chase Donavan, his moods and past. And this troubled her, though she sensed Donavan was a kind man, and up to now he'd treated her civilly. Much to her relief he'd taken a special interest in Jesse, perhaps because her son would be crippled as was her husband in some strange way. On the way out here Donavan had spoken of another place farther to the west. Anything to leave Oklahoma and the bitter memories she still held of Micha Colder.

Some of that bitterness was for how the white man had treated the Cherokee. Even out here her presence with a white man when they'd entered the hotel had drawn scorning looks. Oftentimes the elders of her tribe had told of how the Cherokee had been forced by the United States government to leave their ancestral home in Georgia and make the long journey to the timbered hills and open prairies of eastern Oklahoma, or Indian Territory. The Cherokee were just one of the Five Civilized Tribes forced to immigrate on that "trail of tears" where many had perished. Treaties guaranteed that the Indians would own their lands as long as grass shall grow and rivers run. They cleared land, laid out farms, raised livestock, and built schoolhouses and churches. Each nation established its own laws, built its own capitol in the wilderness, and set up a legislature and courts.

Suddenly the Five Civilized Tribes were forced to decide which side to support when the Civil War broke out. Since they came from the southern states, and

34

some of their leaders were slaveholders, the federal agents of the tribes supported the Confederacy. Even so, some of the Indians fought for the Union. But this made no difference once the Civil War ended, for the federal government ruled that all of the tribes had lost all rights to their lands and treaty guarantees because they had supported the South. Thus it was that the Indian Territory of eastern Oklahoma was thrown open to white settlement. So it came to pass that huge chunks of Cherokee land were lost forever, as was a way of life. Many women of Raven's tribe married white men, or were sold into slavery.

Even now Raven Keepseagle could not blame her father for selling her to that whiskey peddler. But she would never go home again. Always would she retain images of the harsh and unjust Micha Colder. She turned away from the window when Jesse Colder came limping into the room to say that her husband was coming up the staircase.

"Why did you marry this man?" Jesse asked.

Forcing all thoughts of the past away, Raven gazed fondly at her son. Jesse was all she had, and in her was this deep love and concern over what the crippled leg would mean to him upon reaching manhood. At age six, Jesse was too young to understand what had happened. She would never mention the name Micha Colder again. He would come to know Donavan as his father, she hoped.

"Why, Jesse? Because he will give us a new life," She replied.

"Sometimes he scares me."

Crossing to the boy, she placed a comforting arm around his small shoulders. "Do not judge a man by his appearance. Underneath I see kindness . . . and concern for you."

"Why me?"

"Someday, my son, you will understand."

"Am I intruding?" Chase Donavan removed his hat as he passed through the open doorway. In the other hand he carried a parcel wrapped in brown paper and a small brown paper bag. "Jesse, here." He handed the small bag to the boy. "Some candy."

Tossing his hat on a wooden chair, Chase said, "I managed to find a plow . . . and I figure we've got enough other supplies to tide us over for a spell . . . at least until spring."

"Then, we are leaving?"

"In the morning, I expect." Chase Donavan could still remember every detail of the night he'd stumbled upon the Cherokee woman and the boy. There she'd stood, a woman of uncommon beauty, trembling with fear of him yet so desirable in her torn dress. Afterward, at Bartlesville, for some as yet understood reason, he'd lingered to find out what would happen to the boy. Somehow he had become their protector. Or could it have been that Chase had grown weary of this wandering life of a gambler. All he'd associated with were others of his kind: hustlers, bunco artists, the general run of bar girls or worse. There were also the gunfights, for gambling casinos and saloons were sordid places. Inside of Chase Donavan there was still the desire to right what had been done to him by Major James Ramsey, but as time passed, he began to realize he had no leg to stand on, that for all intents and purposes he was the one who'd killed that army sergeant. About all he could do was hunt down that major and exact what revenge he could.

Now he lifted his gaze to Raven's waiting face. "For months the newspapers have been printing stories that the Cherokee Outlet was to be opened for settlement. It didn't mean a whole lot . . . that is, until you came along, Raven. So in the morning, if it's okay with you, we'll head to a place I found a few years back."

"Anyplace will be fine, my husband. Still, Donavan . . . I wonder . . . there are white women who would have found you desirable. . . ."

"I've known a few," he admitted. "And, Raven, where we're going is farther west . . . somewhat isolated. Not much of a social life." He stepped closer and passed to Raven the parcel. "Which is why I'm giving you this."

"A present . . . for me?" She pulled out a velvety blue dress while letting the wrapping flutter to the floor, and in Raven's eyes was a misty kind of happiness.

"Hope it fits."

"It will."

"There's also some other doodads I bought."

"I can wear this lovely dress when we go to church."

"Sooner than that. Tonight there's some doings over at the Grange Hall . . . a dance and such. This is my way of saying I'm mighty proud to have you as my wife." He glanced at Jesse Colder. "Better get washed up, Jesse, 'cause you're going too."

Chapter Three

The new loan officer at the Western Bank in Elk City had about as much authority as a fart in the wind, meaning that any loan authorized by Loren Draeger had to get the final approval of bank president P.T. Milburn. Lately there'd been a lot of folks coming in to borrow money because of the rush westward to buy land. This had caused the bank to raise its prime lending rate and have more money staged over from Oklahoma City. Which set just fine with the sullen-lipped Draeger.

Less than three months ago Draeger, somewhere in his late twenties, had escaped from an Izard County work gang. Before that he'd been a bank teller over at Calico Rock, a small town bordering on the Arkansas Ozarks. The temptation of having all that money pass through his fingers had gotten to Draeger, as had those nightly trysts with the daughter of a wealthy merchant. Then, when Maybelle Turner told him she was in a family way, Loren Draeger decided to break into the bank, only to be apprehended. Draeger could have had his prison sentence commuted if he would have gone into holy wedlock with Maybelle and, after things settled down, been set up in business by her father. The only trouble was the Draegers of Izard County weren't the marrying kind.

It took him around three months to finally wind up at Elk City, on a stolen horse and stone broke. Right off he got a job as a swamper at a local saloon, then gravitated from that to the higher status of being a bardog over at the Broken Elbow Bar. When the ad appeared in the *Elk City Ledger* that the bank needed someone who understood the rudiments of banking, Draeger applied for the job. As he'd done back in Calico Rock, the new loan officer often volunteered to work during the noon hour or do the cleaning up or work late when paperwork piled up.

At the moment, Loren Draeger sat at his desk staring out a window, one hand drumming a pencil, the other scratching at his thinning hairline. To his right was a counting table; beyond that, a big brick stove and pipes spilling out to the heat ducts. Only one teller was working his cage, the two other tellers having left at four o'clock. Opposite was the large iron vault; next to that, P.T. Milburn's office and another large room where meetings were held. The vault door stood open, but would be closed and locked by Milburn once all of the money was put away. Out in the lobby were a few customers and the bank guard, a former cowhand name Rye Haskins. All of these things registered in Draeger's thoughts as he glanced around, then let his gaze slide to the vault. It was in there, over a hundred thousand dollars, in coin and paper money.

"And soon it's gonna be mine" came the soft voice of Loren Draeger.

Slowly he had gained P.T. Milburn's confidence. All along he had thought that the main vault had a time lock, but was told differently just this week. The hard fact was, just across the street from the bank lay the sheriff's office. With the new prosperity coming to Elk City and surrounding towns because of the land rush, the growing population had forced the city fathers to add a couple of deputies, which to Loren Draeger meant robbing the bank could be very hazardous. Long ago he'd discarded this being a solo job. It would take at least five: one to watch the horses, and a lookout, the rest to get in here and get at that vault. So on his nightly sojourns around Elk City and into its saloons and gaming halls, Draeger had searched with a keen eye for the man he wanted.

One look at Matt Traxel a week ago at Billie's Texas Saloon had told him here was somebody special. Draeger had just strode up to the long and crowded bar and propped a boot on the railing when for some reason his eyes were drawn to a man drinking alone at a back table. Gunfighter was stamped all over Traxel's chiseled face, the way he sat there, sort of relaxed but in an alert way, those pale smoky eyes seeming to check out everything that happened around him.

"Ollie, who's the gent back there?"

"Been here going on a couple of days now. I figure he's waiting for somebody."

This proved to be the case when later that evening another gent bearing the stamp of gunhand appeared at the saloon and went back to sit with Matt Traxel. The next day, as Draeger found out from the barkeep over at Billie's Texas Saloon, a couple more hardcases drifted in to associate themselves with Traxel, as did Loren Draeger after finishing his workday at the Western Bank. Back in Izard County he'd known a few moonshiners and petty thieves, but none of them were in the same league with mankillers. His first words to Matt Traxel came out squeaky nervous.

"A business proposition?" Traxel asked.

"Yessir."

"Just what the hell did you say your handle was again?"

"Ah . . . Loren Draeger . . . ah, sir . . . ah Mr. Traxel. . . ."

"How'd you know my name, boy?"

"Found out . . . suh, from a desk clerk at the Butte Hotel."

"Meddlers and fools don't live long in these parts."

Somehow Loren Draeger convinced the gunfighter they could make a lot of money by robbing the Western Bank of Elk City. Over the next few days plans were made to carry this out. Draeger soon learned that Traxel and the other hardcases were rendezvousing here at Elk City before heading west to be hired on by the cattle barons.

"Once this is over," muttered Loren Draeger, "they can go to hell for all I care." He rose when the banker came out of his office.

"Well, Loren, another profitable day."

"Yessuh, Mr. Milburn, it has been. Are you still planning to leave for Oklahoma City on the morning stage?"

"Something came up. So tomorrow for this banker it'll be business as usual."

"For me, also, suh." He watched as the banker closed the door of the vault, trying to conceal his disappointment that P.T. Milburn would still be in town over the weekend They had figured on robbing the bank tomorrow night. During the time he'd been here Draeger had managed to be in position, watching the vault when the banker worked the combination; so Loren Draeger was reasonably certain he had most of the numbers figured out. But why had Milburn changed his mind about leaving? Certainly he hadn't found out that his loan officer had been associating with a few hardcases. Now he tapped on his felt hat and left by the back door. As he went up the alley darkened by the lowering sun, someone called out, "Bank teller . . . over here. . . ."

"Traxel?" He came out of the alley and with some reluctance fell into step with the gunfighter. "I hope nobody saw you."

"Take it easy, boy."

"Mr. Milburn won't be leaving this weekend."

"No matter," said Traxel. "Instead of waiting another day we'll hit the bank tonight. You got any objections to that?"

"Why . . . why the change in plans? It'll be riskier."

"Because this old hoss is tired of hanging around this two-bit town. Come midnight you be waiting out in that alley behind the bank. And if I was you, Draeger, I'd pack my possible bag and have a good horse saddled and standing by."

Matt Traxel lifted out his Navy Colt .45 and spun its cylinder as he surveyed from aboard his black gelding the approaches to the alley. With the gunfighter were three of his breed: capable Sammy Ronyak out of Montana, a blocky man with cynical eyes; Cy Oberbye, a handy man with a running iron; old Ben Sutthill, aging but still damned deadly with either six-gun or long gun. All were men with notches on their guns and cold of heart.

At first Traxel had been amused by that loan officer from the Western Bank seeking him out. He'd arrived in town a day before that, and from long habit he'd checked out the bank, then decided to leave it be since the city jail was located across the street. But he couldn't pass up the golden opportunity presented to him by Draeger. The gunfighter was a slope-shoul-dered and unimposing man in his thirties. The leather cattleman's coat had seen the dust of two summers, though the Stetson was new, and he had on Levi's and spurred Justins. It was to Matt Traxel's advantage that

42

he didn't stand out in a crowd, since more than one witness had difficulty placing a face to the man who'd just robbed a bank or Wells Fargo office. This had changed when the Pinkerton Detective Agency began plastering his picture in newspapers and on telegraph poles and buildings. He'd grown a mustache along with using spectacles having clear lenses. Traxel, as had the others, had been forced to hide out for longer periods of time between jobs. And whenever they did pull a holdup, they left no witnesses.

Traxel had been idling at a whorehouse in Dodge City when a man claiming to represent certain cattle barons found him. Only because one of them, Cy Oberbye, had vouched for the stranger's bona fides did Traxel hire on, to leave immediately and begin the long trek that would eventually take him someplace in the Cherokee Outlet. This time he would get paid to do some killing, a thought now that brought a sparkle into his watchful eyes.

"Maybe that damned bank teller has chickened out," Sutthill complained.

"Maybe so, Ben," Traxel replied.

"Some are like that, all brag and no action."

"But I figure he'll be waiting out behind that bank. Could be we'll get enough to tide us over until spring."

"What about the job we hired on to do?" Sammy asked.

"Those greedy cattle barons need us more'n we need them. But think about it, Sammy, our getting paid to gun down a few nesters . . . and the law on our side."

"My mammy always said I'd make good some day," Sammy agreed.

"Quiet now," cautioned Traxel as he took the point, with the others trailing him up the alley. When the gunfighter spotted Loren Draeger lurking in the recessed doorway, he reined over and slid to the ground.

The others dismounted, and Ben Sutthill took charge of the horses.

"Want I should stand lookout?" Ben asked.

"Won't be necessary," said Traxel. "With Mr. Draeger opening that vault this won't take long."

Opening the back door, Draeger said nervously, "No more talking."

"As you say," Traxel countered.

They hurried through a short back hallway, then veered past the stove and over to the area around the vault, where Draeger motioned toward some money sacks. He pulled a chair over and, easing onto it, placed the fingers of his right hand gently on the round cylinder and began turning it as he sought the right combination. The others clustered nearby, their eyes getting an anxious look whenever Draeger jiggled the round knob, only to come up with a wrong combination of numbers.

"Maybe we use should dynamite—"

"No!" Draeger said loudly. "I'll get it . . . just a little longer. . . ." He worked at turning the knob for another ten minutes, when to his surprise he heard the last tumbler fall into place. Anxiously he grasped the handle and turned it, then strained to open the heavy steel door of the vault.

"Duck soup," exulted Ronyak.

For a brief moment Matt Traxel hesitated as the others shouldered past him toward the vault, his questioning eyes going past the teller windows to the lobby windows. What he'd heard could probably be those leaving a saloon and heading home or a horse trotting past the bank. But years spent on the dodge held Traxel there, his gunhand draping onto the butt of the Navy Colt. Now he was certain trouble had found them when footsteps sounded on the front walkway, followed right away by the rasping of a key in the front door of

44

the Western Bank.

"We've got company!" he rasped out while drawing his handgun. He sprang toward one of the cages. Now through the windows opening onto the street he could make out several cavalrymen strung out behind a U.S. Army payroll wagon. Oftentimes, he knew, payrolls on their way out to frontier outposts were placed in banks for safekeeping until morning, and Traxel cursed away his bad luck as he said, "Take what you've got and head for the horses! 'Cause we've got a lot of company . . . some damned cavalry guarding a payroll wagon. Let's vamoose."

He waved the other hardcases past him and to the back hallway, and when the loan officer Draeger came out holding a money sack, Traxel made a grab for it. "You won't be needing that."

"No . . . I . . . you promised. . . ."

"Only fools and meddlers try to pard up with men on the dodge." Thumbing the hammer back, he shot Loren Draeger in the mouth, the slug punching back to explode brain and skull. He spun and snapped a shot at banker P.T. Milburn, just entering the lobby, to bring a yowl of surprise and pain. Then he was running on his two-inch heels for the hallway and the sanctuary of his horse As he stepped up into the saddle to rein away with the others, he could hear the shouts of cavalrymen reacting to the bitter reports of gunshots. The hardcases pounded out of the alley and away to the west, soon to vanish into the cloudy night.

After a while one of them yelled, "I don't hear nobody behind us!"

"That payroll unit'll be more concerned about what they're protecting," Traxel replied.

"Come morning, though, or maybe sooner, a posse'll be after us."

"By then we'll be long gone."

"We didn't get all that much."

"At least, Oberbye, none of us has any new bullet holes letting in moonlight. Think on the bright side . . . we've got ourselves a job whereby the law protects us whilst we kill sodbusters and the like."

"Something to think about alright, Matt."

"Widow makers," the gunfighter Matt Traxel went on. "That's what we'll be. Widow makers. . . ."

Chapter Four

Northwesterly they ventured to cut across the northern fringes of Texas. The woman and her son Jesse rode in the Conestoga wagon being trundled along by a team of horses, the wagon laden down with all of their possessions and the Hereford bull Chase Donavan had purchased at Elk City plodding reluctantly behind.

Chase rode alongside on his grulla, but more often he'd scout out what lay ahead. Once in a while they'd come across discarded pieces of furniture, the bones of an ox or horse, or a grave marker, mute testimony that some who'd been part of the great land rush opening the Cherokee Outlet had fallen by the wayside. It was a hot August day and would get hotter in the days to come, Chase reckoned. A few hazy clouds littered the high sky, the wind coming hot and out of the southwest, and toward nightfall they reached the Canadian River and a place called Adobe Wells.

Spurring back toward the wagon, Chase said, "Someone's camped down by those trees. Appears to be a small party . . . a sodbuster and his family. Just the same, we'll go in careful."

"Whatever you say, my husband."

"Well, Jesse, are you getting tired of riding?"

When the boy didn't respond, Raven said, "Sometimes my son hides his feelings in silence."

"Something I do a lot," replied Chase. His smile cutting through the collecting darkness, Chase Donavan rode just ahead of the wagon. Closing in, he waved a hand in greeting as those clustered amongst the trees by the river spread out warily. "Hello the camp. Been nearly a week since we've seen a friendly face. Mind if we come in?"

"Be obliged you come in and pitch your camp, stranger."

Raven drove the Conestoga through a cut in the clayey bank and over to a place indicated by her husband. She watched from the wagon seat as Chase slid down and grasped the sodbuster's hand. There it was again in the eyes of the sodbuster and his wife and three children, this silent question of how it was that a white man could pack around a squaw. Suddenly to Raven's surprise the woman broke out in a welcoming smile, then she hurried toward the wagon.

"My dear, you must be dreadfully tired after driving that wagon all day long. Let your husband tend to the horses. There's vittles warming over the fire . . . and hot coffee . . . enough for all of us."

"Why . . . thank you," murmured a grateful Raven Keepseagle. "Come along, Jesse, and meet the children." Rising, she climbed down from the seat and turned back to help her son dismount.

"I'm Clara Purcell."

"Raven . . . Donavan." There had been no marriage rites tying her to Micha Colder. And even now Raven had difficulty using Chase's last name. Perhaps this was all a dream, her being married to Donavan; maybe tomorrow morning she'd wake and find herself still bound to Micha Colder, that heartless man who'd tried to kill his own son. Briefly her eyes took in Chase just starting to unhitch the horses from the Conestoga, as if

48

wanting to reassure herself that he was still here.

"Where did you head out from, Raven?" Clara asked.

"We bought our supplies at Elk City."

"Lordy, I hope they came cheaper than what we had to pay back at Oklahoma City. Those thievin' merchants . . . I do declare. And I suppose you folks are bound for the Outlet?"

"Beyond that." The other children, Raven noticed, seemed to be afraid of her son, the Purcell boys sticking close to their wagon and the girl peering out through a back flap. "Jesse, come and sit by me."

"What happened to your boy's leg?"

"He . . . he fell," said Raven.

"My rascals are accident-prone too. If it isn't some cuts or scratches . . . then it's poison oak or something else. But what was there for us back in Pennsylvania. Just my husband Jacob working at that sawmill . . . and laid off from time to time." Clara Purcell dropped the tailgate, lifted out a couple of chairs and set them by the fire. "My husband made these . . . Jacob's mighty good at working wood. Something that'll come in handy out here . . . that is, if we ever find some choice land."

"We will," called out Jacob Purcell as he moved in alongside Chase Donavan. "Got terribly lucky yesterday and shot a deer . . . one of them muleys. I do hope you folks like venison." Suspenders rode over Purcell's gray woolen shirt and were hooked to corduroy pants, and the felt hat he wore was speckled with dust and stained from sweat. Though lean and a few inches shorter than Chase, he had big farmer's hands, and stubble covered Purcell's angular face. His wife had an ample frame and light brown hair showing under her bonnet.

Right away these people had put Chase Donavan at

49

ease, though when Purcell had helped him unharness the horses, there had been the questioning eyes fixed upon Chase's disfigured face. Then the man had simply made small talk about the weather and how different it was out here. As Chase moved with Jacob Purcell over to a wash basin set on the wagon tailgate, the girl scurried out of the wagon and over to her mother.

"Awful shy little thing." Chase commented.

"Sure don't take after her ma." Jacob smiled at Chase. "You go first."

After both men had washed up, they settled down on the chairs as Clara Purcell ladled food onto plates for her children and Jesse Colder.

"So you're heading up into the Outlet . . ." Chase began.

"Got out here too late for opening day. Probably by now it'll be real tough getting any good land . . . some with water."

"Did you have any particular route picked out?"

"Figured on heading more or less due north." He took the plate of venison stew from his wife and nodded his thanks. "Why?"

"Do that, Jacob, and you'll have to ford three or four rivers."

"That so?"

"Why don't you trail along with us. The route I've got picked out will bring us around most of those rivers and up to the Cimarron Cutoff of the Santa Fe Trail, which is in the western reaches of the Outlet."

"That's mighty hospitable of you, Chase."

"There's always the Indian problem. Traveling together we have a better chance of getting through."

"Heard they" — Jacob Purcell flicked a glance at Raven — "cause trouble at times."

Chase smiled. "My wife is Cherokee . . . and a fine woman."

50

"I can see that," said Purcell.

"You honor us," said Raven, "by sharing your food."

"Ma'am, the pleasure's ours."

First light settled upon their wagons pointing tailgates at the Canadian River fading into the hazy distance. In the days to come they trekked through the Texas counties of Moore, Hartley and Dallam, before Chase announced that the elevation off to the northwest was Rabbit Ear Mountain. Cattle were more plentiful, grazing in bunches on the endless sere plains marked with cacti and juniper and sage brush. At the last waterhole, a spring they'd come upon in an arroyo, the water barrels had been filled, and Chase knew that in not more than two days they would part company with folks he'd come to like.

A day later, as they were approaching the middle fork of the North Canadian River, a rider swung out of a hidden arroyo to lope purposefully toward the wagons. Chase spurred up to Jacob Purcell driving his wagon and said, "Let me do the talking, Jacob."

"Trouble?"

"Probably just some cowpoke out looking for strays."

"Or here to check us out."

Back when he'd been trying to get away from those Coyotero Apache scouts, back in Texas, there'd been the same disdainful look accorded Chase by those Matador cowpunchers, though the man reining up on his bronc was younger. The cowhand hitched at his gunbelt while gazing past Chase at both women riding in the back wagon.

"I'm happy to see your wagon tongue is pointed north," the man commented.

"I've heard it all before, *hombre*," Chase said crisply. "Make it short."

Resentful eyes took in Chase's handgun, and the cowhand hawked tobacco juice at the dusty ground. Some of the spittle caught on his chin, but he didn't seem to notice it. "You must be the squaw man."

"You can't—"

"Easy, Jacob," murmured Chase, and softer, "he isn't alone." Then a casual nod from Chase brought the cowhand looking over his shoulder. "Those your friends?"

"There's—" When the cowhand swiveled his eyes back to the wagons, it was to be confronted with the barrel of Chase Donavan's six-gun pointed at his midriff, with Chase riding in closer.

Chase reined up so that he could almost touch the cowhand's saddle, and he said quietly, "Mister, take a good look at my face. Memorize what you see. Our wagon tongues are pointed north . . . north for Colorado." He reached out and pulled the handgun out of the cowhand's holster and cast it away before tucking the barrel of his gun under the man's bearded chin.

"You just insulted my wife, mister. But then scum like you don't know any different." At the ominous clicking of the hammer when he thumbed it back, the cowhand's eyes gaped wide open, with that disdainful glimmer changing to one of stark terror. Those same eyes took in the burned skin and sightless eye. All the cowhand could do was suck in his gut and let frightened air spill out of his trembling mouth.

Finally he managed to stammer, "There's seven others . . . back there. . . ."

"Since you'll be dead it won't make no difference."

"Please . . . all we was gonna do . . . was hurray you folks some . . ."

". . . tell us this was Circle T or Flying V land . . . that scum like us aren't welcome here. Believe me, mister, your sudden demise won't stir my conscience any.

So here's the way of it. If I let you vamoose . . . all I want to see is eight riders making tracks out of that arroyo and heading away from here. Else you'll be the first to die. *Comprendo?*"

"Sure . . . I'll tell them. . . ."

"First, you owe me an apology."

"What for?"

Pulling the gun away Chase backhanded the cowhand across the face. "To me and my wife. The urge to kill you is still gnawing away, mister."

"I'm . . . sorry . . . real sorry. . . ."

"Death is a black pit . . . for someone like you. Which just can happen if you decide to take out after us. So spin that bronc around and ride."

With the cowhand galloping his bronc away, Chase rode back to the wagons.

Jacob Purcell called down to him, "Don't suppose that gent'll be back."

Swinging down, Chase ground-hitched his reins and said, "Mrs. Purcell, keep an eye on the children . . . and Raven, it just might be that waddy'll be back with his friends. Set the hand brake. Then get down and hold the bridle of the black mare to calm it down in case something happens."

"Lordy," said Clara Purcell, "I don't see how some white men will harm women and children."

"If they do come back, it'll be me and your husband they'll be after." Striding back, Chase opened the tailgate of his Conestoga, then he climbed up and found a rifle enclosed in a doeskin sheath, and shells for the model .50-140-700. This was a newer model of the famous Big Fifty or Sharps 50-100 used by the buffalo hunters. The rifle was part of the booty he'd won in a poker game from a buffer hunter. Instead of packing it around, Chase had left it in the care of a friend over at Broken Arrow, Oklahoma Territory. It came to mind

53

and Chase retrieved it after his marriage to Raven had made up his mind about claiming some land.

He went back to his horse and climbed into the saddle. Cradling the Sharps across his lap as he rode up to Jacob Purcell standing by his wagon, Chase nodded toward a nearby pile of jumbled rocks. "Stand by your wagon, Jacob. Chances are they won't be back until after we pull out. But it could be I riled up that cowpoke's pride something fierce."

"What in tarnation is that thing?"

"Insurance," he said calmly. "That waddy'll be back to retrieve his six-gun. They'll have rifles — Winchesters and maybe Springfields — but not with the range of this Sharps. Once I touch this thing off, Jacob, I figure the odds will even out. Be alert now."

Chase brought his horse into motion, a lope that carried him toward lower ground and westerly, a hundred or so rods to the shelter of rocks. He swung down and settled into a firing place, the Sharps placed on a flat rock, and quickly he loaded a couple of .50 caliber loads into the breech. During his cavalry days Chase had been considered a sharpshooter with the long gun. Afterward, when he'd roamed about Kansas and other places as a gambler, he would take rides out into the countryside and practice with either handgun or rifle. Mostly this was because someday Chase Donavan knew there was to be a reckoning with Major James Ramsey, along with Chase realizing that to stay alive out here a man had to be fairly proficient with a gun. He swung an eye up to the sun and knew that in a little while it would be lowering to come under the brim of his hat and give him trouble.

Then several horsemen appeared, strung out and cantering out of the nearby arroyo, the waddy he'd confronted among them. From where they rode Chase reckoned they could only see the tops of the covered wagons, and then he was squinting down the long barrel of the Sharps. He knew from long experience the cowhands were still out of Winchester range and, knowing this, were riding careless and talking boisterously amongst themselves, that waddy who'd lost his six-gun to Chase gesturing with his arms and seeming to be doing most of the talking.

"Told you not to come back," Chase muttered grimly. It was his intention not to kill the cowhand, but to crease him in the hopes all of them would come to their senses and ride away. One thing about the Sharps, he'd found out from the few times it had been fired, was that it sounded like a freight train clattering over a rocky railbed and, if fired a lot, left the man holding it with a bruised shoulder.

Craaccckkkk!!!

Recoiling from the hard impact of the Sharps, Chase grinned as the big .50 caliber load jerked the cowhand's weathered Stetson away. The others reined up quickly and had to control their wondering horses, and they milled about while trying to locate the source of that strange-sounding rifle. He could see they were hesitating, yet Chase squinted in on another waddy and squeezed off a round. The waddy clutched at his left arm as he almost spilled out of the saddle. One or two broke away, a couple more, then the entire bunch sought the sanctuary of the arroyo. Chase held there until he saw all of them coming up on the western lip and heading away.

He rode back to the wagons to be greeted by Raven's anxious eyes, and he said, "Funny how a rifle that makes a lot of noise can change some minds."

"Did you kill any of them?"

"No need to, Raven. Well, I guess we can get on the move again."

The Purcells came over, and Jacob said, "I doubt if

they'll be back. But that was a brave thing you did, Chase."

"Either that or have to contend with those cowhands. It'll probably happen other places we go — and I don't like it — but that's part of the game being played out here."

Chapter Five

About two days downwind of the Purgatoire River they came upon still another tendril of smoke drifting away from a treeline. Back at Troy, a small settlement farther east on the north fork of the Cimarron, the Purcells had decided to throw in with Chase Donavan's decision to claim land along the Purgatoire River. Throughout the Cherokee Outlet, they'd bypassed the camps of the sodbusters. Chiefly these people had claimed land having water on it, a water hole or creek. And it was pretty much open range country in that Chase hadn't seen any barbed wire fences.

Now he was staring at a drift fence running down from the north and on this side of a nameless creek. Of concern to Chase were the ruts of a wagon passing through a place where the fence had been cut.

"Well, Jacob, that fence was put up by a cattle outfit. I suspect that if we head up thataway we'll find more places where the fence has been cut."

"I don't understand . . . how can these big ranchers claim so much land?"

"By being here first. Which means driving off the Indians and anybody else."

"Does this mean whoever put up that fence also lays claim to that creek?"

"That's about it, Jacob."

"It seems we have a decision to make, my friend Donavan."

"Yup . . . suppose so. This fence could stretch for miles in either direction, north or south. And where we're goin' is thataway."

"That smoke . . . could it be one of those cow camps?"

"Probably that nester who cut this section of fence. Only one way to find out."

With a confident wink for the Purcells seated in their wagon, Chase rode back to his and swung to the ground. He told Raven that he would bring the wagon through the gap in the fence and ford it across the creek, and then he helped her down, feeling the closeness and woman scent of this beautiful woman who'd married him.

In her eyes was an unmasked concern as Raven said, "There could be trouble. . . ."

"Always that out here. But it isn't that far to the Purgatoire, another day at the most. That's just more nester smoke yonder."

"Yes, my husband, I feel it is." She found the reins and the saddle of Chase's horse.

Donavan, Raven's son Jesse eying him from the opposite side of the wide wagon seat, brought the wagon through the fence and along a stretch of rough prairie land settling into cracked loamy ground forming part of the creek bed. There was only a trickle of water, so crossing proved to be a minor difficulty. The smoke, as Chase had determined, came from a campfire made by a family of nesters: a man and his wife and two strapping sons. He tipped his hat in response to a half-hearted wave from the nester.

"Don't worry, mister, you won't have us for neighbors." Several trees had been felled, and some formed

58

the lower reaches of a log cabin, though it was Chase's strong opinion that the rancher claiming this land would retaliate for his fence being cut by either killing the nestor or sending him packing.

Would it be any different farther west along the Purgatoire? There it was mostly Hispanics from Mexico who'd established settlements or plazas, several families banding together under the direction of their patron. These people led a simple life, raising goats and chickens and having a few milk cows while the men worked for local ranchers. As he'd explained to Raven and the Purcells, it was Chase's intention to start a small farm and later to branch out into ranching. Another reason for his returning, and Chase had kept quiet about this, was to see again that place where patron Hilario Madrid had found him. The night of that terrible lightning storm would always be etched in his thoughts. Afterward, he had bid *adios* to the Madrids and scouted out the hogback positioned just west of the river to find fertile bottomland. It had proved to have a few bluffs, plenty of woodland and a spring or two located between Van Bremer arroyo and the cowtown of Trinidad. Cattle roamed freely through this large parcel of land as did game animals. At that time — could it be going on seven years — there'd been no restricting barbed wire fences. Again, maybe the land he sought had been claimed by others. Through his musings about the place Chase Donavan had this notion it was still unclaimed land.

Underbrush tore at the wagons going up humpy land spread along the Purgatoire, which was composed of a deep watery channel. By dead reckoning, Chase had angled to the northwest ever since leaving that last stream two days ago to come upon the middle reaches of the river he sought. Spurring ahead, he scared out an old mossback bull, which snorted its displeasure before catching a scent of the Hereford tied to Chase's wagon. The mossback bellowed a challenge, and then shook its head and shambled away. Clearing the brush, Chase laid an eager eye upon a place he'd seen seven years ago, the openings to Red Rock Canyon and the home of Hilario Madrid and other Hispanics.

"Upstream a quarter of a mile there'll be a ford," Donavan pointed out.

"I see some buildings over there," said Clara Purcell.

"The plaza of Hilario Madrid."

"Will we be welcomed?"

"Let's find out."

"Someone has seen us."

Chase stared opposite at a young man striding away from an adobe building, and he said, "One of Hilario's sons."

They brought the wagons farther north to the watery crossing, and Chase smiled at the anxious look on Raven's face. He said, "The river bottom is a little rocky but safe for crossing. If you don't have the gumption to—"

"I have driven this far," snapped Raven. "So what is one more river crossing." Her even rows of teeth bared in a determined smile, she reined the pair of horses pulling her wagon down the sloping bank ahead of the other wagon, with Chase Donavan riding alongside. "Go ahead, my husband, I do not need a babysitter."

"Suit yourself," said Chase as he spurred onward. Splashing across, he drew up on the western bank and folded his hands over the saddle horn, watching as Raven brought their wagon across and more people began drifting toward them from the Hispanic settlement. Some men on horseback broke through those on foot, and Chase recognized a man named Felipe Cortez and the patron himself, Madrid.

Only when Chase swung his horse to the south did Hilario Madrid cry out, "Can it really be you, Donavan?"

"*Si,* Hilario, it is none other."

The former cavalry officer and the man who'd saved him came down off their horses and embraced, and stepping away, the patron shouted, "This calls for a *celebración. Si . . . vamos a celebrarlo. Ustedes . . .* Carlos, Manuel . . . make ready the barbecue pit — and there shall be dancing to *celebrar* the return of El Condor."

That name conjured up for Chase Donavan the days and weeks he'd spent here recovering from his wounds. There were moments when he lay on a bed in Hilario Madrid's abode house that his only salvation was the thought of finding a gun and ending his life. To be hideously marked like this meant that he would be shunned wherever he rode. Though his wounds healed, inwardly there were deep scars. But after a while the patron Madrid, sensing the anguish tearing at Chase, would draw him into quiet conversation. In shattered fragments he drew out of Chase his tale of betrayal. That place, the hogback, Hilario Madrid had narrated, was the adobe of the spirits, and these spirits unleashed their swift and terrible swords during summer storms. Only the mighty condor, Madrid went on, could survive this fiery onslaught, and so Chase Donavan became known as the Condor to these deeply religious and superstitious people.

He couldn't help noticing that Hilario Madrid had aged, the coal-black hair more gray-streaked and deeper lines in the seamed face under the old sombrero. And Madrid's two sons had become men. As he and the patron moved over to the wagon, Chase introduced, "My wife, Raven . . . and Jesse."

"*Que dia tan, señora. Si,* my friend, *es una belleza.*"

Around a pleased smile Chase said, "Yes, my wife is beautiful." He gestured at Jacob Purcell and his wife coming toward them. "These are the Purcells, Hilario—Jacob and Clara. Come out here to find themselves a new home."

Duffing his sombrero, the patron gestured with it at the others who'd come out from the small settlement. "*Señor* and *señora* . . . I welcome you on behalf of *todos* . . . of everyone. Come, bring your wagons into our little village. For all of you it must have been a . . . a long *viaje por mar*."

"Yup, they came a heap farther than I did," said Chase.

Venturing along the riverbank with the others, Chase noticed the small plaza was unchanged, the few adobe houses and those of jacal, these composed of piñon posts filled with mud, standing under shading trees, and the small garden plots extending well into the canyon. The ground before Madrid's larger adobe house was barren, and chickens scattered away at their approach. Since most of the men weren't around, Chase assumed they were working as usual out at local ranches.

Cutting past the buildings was the irrigation ditch that had been under construction when he'd been here, and Chase recalled how the men had used crude wooden shovels to hack away at the hard ground. The ditch was very crooked and about ten feet deep and around three wide. In making it the Hispanics had let the water run ahead in the ditch to see if they needed to dig deeper, and working in this way the task had taken around three months. Upon its completion came the harder task of plowing their small fields. Their plows were hewed out of forks of trees. The points for the plows were fashioned out of pieces of iron that the men had sharpened on a rock and nailed to the wood.

With these crude instruments, they somehow raised bountiful crops of wheat, melons, beans, pumpkins, and chili. These fields, of no more than four acres, were reaped each year with hand scyths. Then the wheat was thrown onto a cleared space among the buildings and watered down before the children and goats and sheep went round and round trampling the wheat until it was thrashed. This had been a pleasant time for Chase, that autumn of seven years ago. And it was one of the memories that had brought him back.

"Still," he murmured silently, "things must have changed in seven years. . . ."

"*Si*, many things have changed," Hilario said as they relaxed after dinner.

Some of the men of the village and the new arrivals sat on the covered porch extending along the adobe wall. No wind stirred the trees in the canyon, and the heat of day still lingered in the muted night air. A few children, those of the sons of Hilario Madrid, ran around the house playing tag. Since the moon was full, no lantern had been lighted. Chase's cigarette glowed brightly in the darkness when he dragged on it.

Hilario Madrid went on. "More people — those of your race — have settled along the river. The grande ranchers resent this. Where I work, the H-L Ranch, there is talk of bringing in hired guns."

"*Eso es verdad*," intoned another.

And Madrid added, "This situation . . . this *esto me alarma*." Sadness gleamed in the patron's crinkled eyes. "These ranchers have such a lust for land . . . so much land." He went on to tell of how the ranchers followed the common practice of controlling large portions of the public domain by securing ownership to the important water locations. Thus others could not use the range because their stock would have no access to water. "Now has come the accursed barbed wire . . . stringing fences around water holes . . . fences that extend beyond what a man can ride in a day . . . fences that bring death to cattle and wild animals alike."

"Two winters ago," continued Hilario, "a terrible storm swept out of the Rockies . . . out of the northwest. It drove many cattle before it, antelope, deer, other wild creatures. Across the open prairie they were forced by this blizzard, only to encounter the first of many barbed wire fences. Upon encountering this strange barrier they became confused. They massed together before it . . . huddling there and dying when being overwhelmed by the storm. Farther south, in Texas, there was a fence a hundred miles long . . . and after the storm was over, along its entire length could be found the carcasses of thousands of cattle and other animals. A horrible end; a sad end."

"I recollect that happening," Chase said. "Barbed wire can be a two-headed monster — sometimes beneficial, or destructive if not used properly. What about that land south of here?"

"I felt you would ask about that," the patron said softly. "That it would draw you back, El Condor. *Si*, there is unclaimed land south of Van Bremer Arroyo. There is one other thing. . . ."

"And what is that, Hilario?"

"It is what I found out in Trinidad. Some foreigners have come in and offered to buy out any rancher who wants to sell. So far these Scotsmen have bought the Cross L Ranch and the LIT spread."

"And some ranches farther north along the Purgatoire," said a village elder.

"*Si*, agreed Madrid. "And at Trinidad I saw some wagonloads of barbed wire were also purchased by the Prairie Cattle Company."

"These Scotsmen must have a lot of money," said Jacob Purcell. "All I want is some land to homestead on."

"Have they offered to buy some of your land, Hilario?"

"As yet, no, Donavan. But they can . . . *vayase a la porra!* — go to the devil!"

"Sometimes we see men riding for the Prairie Cattle Company on the other side of the river," said Abeyta, one of the older men. "This is mostly at night; afterward we hear that a murder has been committed or someone burned out. But they leave us alone because we are no threat to them."

The patron said worriedly, "These are greedy men, I'm afraid. There are many plazas such as ours along this river. Perhaps too many. One day they might decide they want what has taken us years to build up. *Si* . . . what then, my friends?"

"We must say a few prayers."

"*Si*, I pray," said Hilario Madrid, "but out here the Bible is no match for the gun. So I pray all the harder."

"It's coming onto autumn," Chase reflected. "Hardly the time to be starting a homestead."

"We'll just be lucky to build our cabins," said Jacob Purcell.

"When the time comes," said Madrid, "we will help."

"I owe you more'n my life, Hilario."

"We are friends, El Condor. Only by standing together can we keep our lands."

Chapter Six

The weather stayed warm but windy throughout autumn, a time during which Chase Donavan claimed land along the Purgatoire where it bent to the west, then continued on for about five miles before curling southward toward Trinidad. There were plenty of oak and cottonwoods, and berries such as chokecherry and blackberry grew in the thick underbrush. In an arbor framed by oak trees, he'd made his camp, with the hogback a distant backdrop and a grassy meadow stretching toward the river. Next year, if they survived the winter to come, there'd be a log house, sheds, and another corral.

Ever since coming here the Donavans had been sleeping alongside the wagon in a tent. During the shortening days Chase had cut down and hauled in piñon posts for the temporary house he planned to build. For a man more used to rifling a deck of cards the hard work had thinned him out, toughened up his hands, and made him appreciate more the coming of night and a hot meal prepared by Raven. He knew the Purcells, who'd claimed land on the opposite side of the river and up north about five miles, would be having an equally hard time of it. The work on the house had gone slow for Chase until earlier in the day Hilario

Madrid and some of his neighbors had come riding in. They's also brought along some women to help Raven with the cooking as well as a packhorse laden down with supplies.

Under the capable hands of his new neighbors the house quickly took shape, the walls and roof beams going up. The patron said that tomorrow a suitable roof would be laid. While just before dusk in rode the Purcells.

"Mr. Madrid stopped by on his way down here," explained Jacob Purcell. "So tell me, Chase, what do you know of woodworking?"

"Not a whole lot," he had to admit.

"Fair enough," Purcell said, "Fetched some tools along; come morning I'll make some windows and doors, do the framing. And, Hilario, I sure do appreciate you volunteering to stop at my place afterward and help on my new house."

"But what are *vecinos* for?" Hilario Madrid duffed his hat and gazed to the south at more meadowland stretching away from the river. "This is good bottomland, Donavan. But farther away from the river it will be necessary to make an irrigation ditch."

"Well, Hilario, I'll plow up some of it. But if the market price for cattle stays up, I might just do some ranching."

"Which is one reason I came here, my friend," said Madrid.

"You speaking of that Hereford bull?"

"*Sí*. We have cattle . . . not many . . . but that bull of yours could give them some fine calves."

"Raven's waving at us to head over to supper. Reckon we could work out something since I'll be needing some cattle before winter socks in."

"What does a bull like that cost?"

"Plenty."

67

"The ranch where I work has bulls like that. They produce beefier calves than do Longhorns. But, alas, my neighbors and I cannot afford such a luxury."

The evening meal was a long and enjoyable affair. Afterward the men stayed seated in the leafy arbor sipping from glasses of brandy while one of the Hispanics played a few Spanish songs on his guitar. After each song there was polite applause from the men, for the women were clustered in a group off to one side, and every so often Chase glanced over at the new house where Jesse Keepseagle was playing with the Purcell children. Down here the boy had become his silent companion. To Chase it was as if they'd signed some unwritten pact whereby neither of them would discuss their pasts.

"Have you gone up there?" Hilario broke into Chase's thoughts.

For a long time Chase gazed into the patrón's wondering eyes. Madrid, he knew, was talking about the mysterious hogback, that hump of land to the northwest marking one boundary of his land. The third day after coming Chase Donavan had saddled up and ridden out alone. After a half-day's ride had brought him to an arroyo, he'd drawn up on one rim and looked to the southeast to the wending course of the Purgatoire. Down by the river was where those scouts from Fort Randall had crossed, with him barely ahead and riding for his life. Here was the arroyo, and yonder the hogback, drenched that stormy night by torrential rain . . . the target of massive lightning bolts . . . a place where Chase had expected to die.

He rode down into the arroyo and beyond, over rising and falling terrain. The wind was cooler than yesterday and had in it a warning that colder weather was on the way. Then he brought his horse around a blocking jumble of rocky land and gazed upon the strange

68

formation capped by crumbling rocks stacked there a long time ago. It took Chase the rest of the day to find the bony remains of his horse, the rotting saddle and that one iron shoe exploded away by lighting. Under sunlight he found that the rocks forming the hogback were unmistakably that of iron content.

As he stood holding the reins of his horse, Chase touched what the lightning had done to his face. Within him still burned a bitter resentment toward Major James Ramsey. A few discreet inquiries by Chase had revealed that Ramsey had been reassigned to another army post. Probably by now, he mused, Ramsey was due for retirement or, recalling how the man operated, had advanced to the rank of colonel or general. Long ago Chase had discarded any thoughts of giving himself up to military authorities. Or of even trying to pick up the threads of his army career. To do so meant he would have to come up with something against James Ramsey, and he didn't have a leg to stand on.

"Anyway . . . now there's Raven. . . ."

At first Chase had suspected that she'd married him only to give Jesse a home. He'd accepted that. But for Chase Donavan it had been a feeling that Raven was very special, a woman whose beauty seemed to grow, even out here in this Colorado wilderness. How was it though, he asked, that even someone like Raven Keepseagle could live with a man scarred of face as he was. They hadn't spoken of love for one another, during courting or afterward. He supposed the cold fact was that they needed each other, two people reeling from what life had done to them, now defiantly striking back at the unfairness of it all. He'd found she was capable, tender of heart, a woman who just might expect more out of life than he could give her. And one thing was for damned certain, Raven Keepseagle deserved that, and probably more. Chase knew he was a lucky man.

Bringing his thoughts back to the present, Chase finally said in response to the man's question, "I have Hilario. Found my horse too."

"None of my people ever venture there." Hilario Madrid shrugged and smiled. "Superstition, perhaps. Or perhaps out of respect for . . . *Sabe Dios.*"

"That could be."

'I have a feeling too, El Condor, that it will save your life again."

In the morning along the wending river road, passing on the other side of the Purgatoire appeared a peddler in his clattering wagon. The peddler reined up and shouted, "Hello the camp! Where you folks hail from?"

"It is I . . . Hilario Madrid. Cross over and we might buy something, Señor Higbee."

Chase backed up his team of horses to bring slack into the chain wrapped around some posts as the peddler brought his wagon down a cut in the bank. Unlike Jacob Purcell, Chase was building well away from the road, mostly because he didn't want any unwelcome visitors dropping in. There was always the possibility someone from his army days would be traveling through these parts. Also, Fort Lyon was farther north where the Arkansas River joined with the Purgatoire. Last week he'd sighted a cavalry patrol passing along the road, and his inquiries about it to Hilario revealed this was an unusual event down here, that perhaps the army had business farther south at Trinidad. Though he'd adopted western ways and mannerisms, Chase still couldn't shake the wary habits picked up while on the dodge. They'd become engrained into him, as had the way he could handle a rifle or mule things over for a longer time. Rashness, haste, quick judgments, once he'd wore all of these hats, and more. At the moment he couldn't help thinking that he owed this change of attitude to the man who'd wronged him.

"Hello the house!"

"*Como esta Ud,* Señor Higbee?"

"Fit as a fiddle, Madrid. Fat and saucy and fit as a fiddle. And who might you be, stranger, to be building this lovely palace out here?"

"Someone looking for roots." Chase smiled. "What else you got besides pots and pans and such?"

"An invention that will change the course of human endeavor!" exulted the peddler as he heaved off the seat and jumped down. Under the open waistcoat could be seen a blazing red vest across which a watch chain described a drooping arc, and the peddler had on a weathered black tophat decorated with an ornamental Indian band, his long and snaggly hair falling upon bulging shoulders and almost to his large waistline. Madrid and the other men clustered around as the peddler opened the tailgate. "Yes, friends, see what modern invention has wrought." Heaving out a sewing machine, he set it down and swung an arm at Chase Donavan.

"A new house needs something to break the hard labors of a wife. This will not only do that, mister, but give you plenty of clothing to boot."

"Gee"—Chase shrugged—"thought you was selling saddles and such."

"Is it . . . something for the blacksmith shop?" Hilario asked.

"No, Madrid, this here's the finest sewing machine on the market, bar none, I wager."

"A *mujer's* toy," the patron said scornfully.

"Just where is your missus . . . ah, there she is—"

"That's Jacob's wife."

"Ah, yes," the peddler said hesitantly, "the dark-haired woman. A fair damsel . . . Mr. . . ."

"Name's Donavan."

"Along with this marvel of efficiency, Mr. Donavan, I'll throw in several spools of thread . . . and a bolt of the finest cloth—burlap—it'll stand up to most anything if made into pants or a shirt or two."

"Well," murmured Chase, "just don't know. You come up through Trinidad?"

"I did, sir."

"And how are things there?" broke in Madrid.

"Well, Madrid, tempers are boiling between your people and the other townsfolk."

"That has happened before, Señor Higbee."

"Too many Mexicanos are being arrested without cause . . . or even due process of law. Now there's been a shooting—some damnfool deputy down there winged a Mexicano kid over some petty thieving."

"Such is life."

"I suppose so," the peddler went on, "but now this big cattle company has come in and laid down some awful foolish new rules for everyone to follow. According to all the bar talk the law in Trinidad has sold out to this cattle company. That ain't all, I'm afraid. Mr. Donavan, it seems folks like you comin' out here to homestead are actually trespassers . . . that is, according to this new cattle company. There's gonna be trouble . . . and this here child don't want'a be anywhere in the neighborhood when it breaks out. So, Mister Donavan, still interested in purchasing this sewing machine?"

"It seems like an awful expensive investment."

"An investment in the future, I assure you, sir. Forty dollars just seems like a lot of money."

"Thirty's a fair price."

"Come now, Mr. Donavan, a machine like this . . .

72

why—"

"Thirty . . . and another silver dollar thrown in to seal the deal."

"What can one do against one such as this, Madrid. Very well, thirty-one is it, along with the other pediments I mentioned."

"You bought this . . . for me?" Raven asked.

Chase swung around to look at his wife staring at the sewing machine in disbelief. For a moment he didn't know what to say. But that look of wonderment in Raven's eyes brought him to her side. "The Lord knows we'll need clothes out here. I . . . I wish there was more I could give you. Like one of those cast-iron stoves we saw back at Oklahoma City. Or maybe a better life than this."

Then, and much to Chase Donavan's surprise, the woman he'd married pressed her lips against his cheek and said quietly, "You have given me life, my husband."

Chapter Seven

The trouble in Trinidad started a couple of months before over a stage driver name Frank Blue breaking the leg of a Mexican in a wrestling match. So when some angry Hispanics came after Blue, he pulled out his Peacemaker and killed Pablo Martinez. Blue was caught and put under protective custody. The next evening a few Anglo friends forced Deputy Sheriff Juan Tafoya to release Blue, and Blue and his rescuers took refuge in Philo Sherman's Colorado Hotel. Gunfire broke out on both sides, with more Anglos holing up at the Colorado Hotel and exchanging gunfire with some three hundred Hispanics led by Sheriff Juan N. Guiterrez. When Blue and several others made their escape, the remaining Anglos in the hotel surrendered. The ringleaders were jailed, but fearing the wrath of the Hispanics, the station keeper at the Hole-in-the-Prairie stage stop sent a wire to Fort Lyon. So it was that a rescue party under the command of Colonel James Ramsey made a hasty march to Trinidad. With the army in town, the uproar over the killing of Pablo Martinez soon died down.

The summer passed quietly, though with some concern the Hispanics found themselves rubbing elbows with the men working for the Prairie Cattle Company.

The company set up its headquarters in Trinidad, that in the form of a new building on the south end of main street. For a while two Scotsmen were in town overseeing the operation, but as summer ran its course one of them left. No sooner had dust from the departing stagecoach died away than Ian MacGregor sent out word that he was hiring men able to handle a gun. Along with this, freighters began bringing in the telegraph poles and wire and wagonloads of barbed wire and posts to hook it to, while the land office in Trinidad saw many a landowner coming in to sell his land to Ian MacGregor's cattle company. The laborers were hired to string fence lines around waterholes and streams, and to put up telegraph lines connecting the varying outposts of MacGregor's company with Trinidad. With the approach of winter the Prairie Cattle Company had enclosed one million acres of public domain in Colorado. Included in this acreage were small homesteads and cattle along the Purgatoire River.

With much concern the sheriff of Trinidad had watched his town slowly being taken over by the Anglos. Guiterrez could understand ambition, the desire to buy land, but not of the scope being used by the Scotsman Ian MacGregor. Now the hard-eyed men were drifting in. It took little imagination on his part to know these men were here at the behest of the Prairie Cattle Company. Soon there would be killings. Although Trinidad was county seat of Las Animas County, there was little money in its coffers to hire extra deputies. That is, until Ian MacGregor had gotten together with the county commissioners and offered to pay the salaries of any men hired to wear a deputy badge. "But," MacGregor had insisted, "they must be men I select."

At the moment Sheriff Guiterrez was gazing sourly

at the few coffee grounds left in his tin cup as he stood in the open doorway of the town jail. Morning sunlight was just touching upon main street. A hazy red rode along the eastern skyline, and no clouds were showing. The Mexican influence showed in many adobe buildings lining the street. Many of these were business places belonging to American traders, along with some billiard-saloons and boardinghouses. Strong drinks were sold at every one of these establishments, a habit that commenced before breakfast, continuing all day and really picking up at sunset. Those with considerable influence or hard cash—the bigger ranchers, businessmen, politicians and the county judge—hung out at the bar in the Colorado Hotel. Since Trinidad lay along the upper reaches of the Santa Fe Trail, every day saw strangers passing through, with many of them availing themselves of the whores at either Spike Reeve's Starlight Casino or a boardinghouse run by a woman who'd once lived in Chicago. But it was the sheriff's firm opinion that you could catch a social disease at either place.

"Serves these Anglos right," he muttered, this more to himself than to his deputy Tafoya, who was just lifting the coffeepot from the round pot-bellied stove. Guiterrez swung the door shut and found the swivel chair behind his cluttered desk. He stared up at Tafoya refilling his cup.

"I don't like it either, Juan, the county hiring three new deputies."

"Three Anglos who'll do what the Scotsman asks."

"Don't you have authority to fire them?"

"*Autoridad?* About all I have is over my own bladder."

"What about Halloran?"

"The esteemed Judge Darcy Halloran has sold out to that cattle company," Guiterrez said bitterly.

"Are you *seguro?*"

"All that ever happened here before MacGregor arrived were a few fights . . . knifings . . . or petty thievery. Not enough to arouse the interest of Darcy Halloran. Now there's money to be made for those who side with MacGregor. Halloran is nobody's fool; he'll do whatever that cattle company wants to expand its interests. Why do you *pensar,* Tafoya, that MacGregor wanted those extra deputies?"

"For *seguro* the Scotsman is a greedy man. . . ."

"One of the clerks over at the courthouse told of how our judge gave MacGregor a briefcase filled with quit-claim deeds."

"I *comprender.*" Tafoya scowled. "Whoever does not sell his land to the deputies of MacGregor will find themselves in grave danger."

"The deputies will be no threat."

"Those others?"

"*Si,* those such as Matt Traxel and the men riding with him. If a rancher or nester . . . or even friends of ours do not take up MacGregor's miserly offer . . . there will be gunplay."

"What can we do?"

"Try to keep from getting killed while this is going on. To keep law and order the best we can. But I fear, Tafoya, there are too many of them." Sighing, all Sheriff Guiterrez could do was to sit there and watch the deputy suck worriedly at his yellow-stained teeth. He shoved the cup away, thinking of the others who'd been drifting into Trinidad this past week, a gathering of cattle barons summoned here by Ian MacGregor.

"Tafoya, watch the office," he said gruffly. Unlike his Mexican deputies, the sheriff wore a dark brown cattleman's hat. He wore a leather vest, his one gun, a Navy Colt, dangling at Sheriff Guiterrez's right hip, the dark trousers hanging over the scuffed boots. The square and tanned face rarely showed emotion, but the dark brown eyes of the middle-aged Hispanic showed an unmasked concern for all that was happening.

The morning sun hammered at Guiterrez as he crossed over and moved along the street, drumming to the sound of a passing freight wagon. Out in front of a cantina the sheriff stayed his hand from reaching to open the door as a Barlow & Sanderson stagecoach swung onto the street. At a lope the driver brought his six horses past Guiterrez. Veering toward the Colorado Hotel, the stagecoach pulled up, and with some interest the sheriff watched the three passengers dismount: a liquor salesman whom Guiterrez recognized, a cowpuncher being handed his saddle by the shotgun, lastly a dapper man being greeted by none other than Ian MacGregor.

"Seen this *hombre* before?" puzzled Sheriff Guiterrez. And right here in Trinidad, but it was difficult for him to see the stranger's features the way the morning sun kept glaring over the buildings. "*Si* . . . the way he walks . . . like a soldier. That colonel from Fort Lyon, Ramsey." It must have been something of a personal nature that had brought the colonel down here, though Guiterrez had the uneasy feeling Ramsey was here by special invitation of the Prairie Cattle Company.

He sought a table in the cantina, and after ordering something to eat, the thoughts of Sheriff Guiterrez went to the last time Colonel James Ramsey had been in Trinidad. This had been when the man Blue had gunned down an Hispanic. About the colonel had been this cold disdain for the Mexicans living down here, and Guiterrez himself. If trouble came again, Ramsey had as much as told him, don't expect any help from Fort Lyon.

78

Bringing a troubled hand up to brush away a lock of errant black hair, Sheriff Guiterrez muttered. "Before long much blood will be spilled. Both the Anglos and my people."

"Colonel, I can make you a very rich man."

"Or I'll spend some time at Leavenworth."

"Not if we handle this properly," countered Ian Mac-Gregor. "The other ranchers I've asked to come here agree with my assessment of the situation. How do you Americans say it . . . the squeaky wheel gets the grease?"

Colonel James Ramsey sipped thoughtfully from his glass as the Scotsman opened a humidor and selected a cigar. He had just been offered more money than he'd earned during his last ten years of soldiering. By now there should have been at least one star adorning his epaulets. It was with a great deal of displeasure that he'd accepted the transfer to Fort Lyon, knowing that his being sent there meant he was being shunted aside in favor of younger officers. A year from now he would be asked to retire. This would be an inglorious ending to his military career. At age forty-five James Ramsey knew he couldn't live on the meager pension he would receive, nor was there too much money saved up. Like it or not, he had little choice but to accept MacGregor's offer.

MacGregor spoke again. "As for that squeaky wheel, Colonel Ramsey, we have paid a lot of money to our representatives in Washington, asking them not to pass new legislation for this territory."

"A law," said Ramsey, "that would give the president authority to remove enclosures on public land restricting the settlement of the area. If passed, you and the other ranchers would have to tear down your illegal fences."

"That's why we need your help, sir."

"That being to look the other way when something happens to a homesteader or small rancher. Of course you're speaking of . . . murder. . . ."

"This is a cruel business in a cruel land, Colonel Ramsey. What we are speaking of are millions of dollars; more importantly, power. You have this as commandant of Fort Lyon. An order from you, and troopers of your Seventh Calvary carry it out without question. As my men will do when the time comes. Colorado is far removed from the Nation's capital . . . to some a distant planet where gunplay is the order of the day."

Ian MacGregor, a tall, thin and sandy-haired man, took out his pocket watch. He was dressed elegantly in cotton trousers, a waistcoat and a brocaded shirt and string tie. The face was long with thin hips and a bulging forehead above penetrating blue eyes. "Almost time for the meeting to start, Colonel Ramsey. So will you throw in with us?"

"Seems I cannot refuse your tempting offer, MacGregor. But make no mistake about this, sir, betray me and I will have your head."

"Egad"—MacGregor smiled—"already we speak of betrayal. No, my friend, there is too much at stake here. And you underestimate yourself, Colonel Ramsey, for without your help our endeavor would be doomed to failure."

"Perhaps I'm not getting enough for my services?"

"Twenty thousand for starters, a tidy sum. Enough to buy some land for yourself. Or simply let it draw interest in a Denver bank. There'll be more coming your way, Colonel."

"Money that will make me a party to murder." A pensive smile showed on Colonel James Ramsey's blocky face as he reached back in his memory to a fort down in Texas and the man he'd framed for murder, Chase Donavan. He was once a murderer, so what would happen up here in Colorado caused no stir of conscience. "But, MacGregor, as you said, a price must be paid if one aspires to become rich."

Chapter Eight

This coming weekend Sergeant Burl Adamle's leave would be over, and he wasn't looking forward to returning to his duties at Fort Lyon. Adamle had another year to go on a three-year reenlistment, but just thinking of leaving Marie Cordova back here at Trinidad had gotten him to ponder over deserting. This was peacetime, and hell, a lot of other soldiers had gone over the wall.

Sergeant Adamle's first visit to this comfortable Hispanic cowtown had been earlier this summer. They'd been summoned here to help the local sheriff calm down matters between the Anglos and the Hispanics, a stay that had dragged out to almost a month. Some of the troopers, including Adamle, had been invited to a local dance. And there he'd seen her, Marie Cordova. Around here the Mexican girls married young, so Burl Adamle was surprised to find that Marie at twenty-four hadn't tied the knot yet. Somehow he wrangled an invitation to her home, which was where Adamle could be found most evenings after that. Another surprise was his behavior around Marie, for he was more accustomed to rough and tumble bar girls. He'd even felt embarrassed kissing her, wanting more than that, promising to return and do some serious courting.

Adamle had rented a room at one of the boarding-houses. Since Marie worked as a housekeeper, days would find him haunting the saloons. His favorite had become Joe Pike's Bar and its poker tables. These were chiefly quarter limit games, steep enough for the locals and a man drawing sergeant's pay. But the beer came out cold and frosty from the tap at the long bar, and today Burl Adamle had just taken the measure of some cowhands at poker.

"Sergeant, with your luck you should quit soldiering and run for public office." The waddy said this in a bantering way.

"Yup, if I can find enough idiots to vote me into office. Been meaning to ask, just what does bring all you lazy cowpunchers into town anyway?"

"Seeing as how you're buying, I'll overlook that insult." The waddy set his beer stein down on the bar and said more guardedly, "I work for the Circle Diamond. Chet there, another big outfit, the XIT. It boils down to that our bosses are in town for a powwow. They aim to make war on those coming in and claiming land around our waterholes and creeks and such."

"I saw all them wagons heading out loaded with barbed wire."

"Courtesy of the Prairie Cattle Company."

"What about this Homestead Act? Doesn't that give nesters the right to claim one hundred sixty acres and found—"

"It boils down to who was here first, Sergeant. Hell, all of us have fought Indians. Saw a few of my friends go under. This is cattle country, pure and simple. Let them that think otherwise beware."

With the departure of the cowhands, Adamle glanced from where he stood at the bar out the front window. He could see upstreet and the Colorado Hotel. Much to his surprise he'd spotted Colonel James Ramsey arriving on the stage. It was is bad luck that Ramsey had been sent out to Fort Lyon. He could still remember those Apache scouts reporting back to Fort Randall with the news of Chase Donavan's demise. Adamle had been a corporal then, and was probably the only living witness to the murder of Sergeant Matt Riddell. This was the reason he'd busted the lieutenant out of that stockade. Seven years later it seemed both of them had changed, Colonel Ramsey packing more weight but with the same cynical disposition, and Burl Adamle graying so that he packed a gray handlebar mustache and had gray hair laying thick at his temples. Up at Fort Lyon he kept clear of Ramsey, for in the man's eyes Adamle had glimpsed a haunted look as of someone always looking over his shoulder at the past. A man like that wouldn't hesitate to kill anyone coming against him.

"Well . . . another year of this mule crap and Burl Adamle is done soldiering," he mused.

He went outside and sauntered down the street. There was something about Trinidad that had gotten to him. This just might be a place to settle in with Marie. Homesteading had no appeal to a man accustomed to riding all day long, nor did hooking on as a cowpoke, for that meant low wages and longer hours saddlebound. Just past nooning Main Street was crowded with those afoot using the boardwalks. He wasn't all that hungry, but force of habit brought Adamle crossing to enter a small cafe. Because all they served at the Cordvas was Mex food, he ordered a hot beef sandwich and coffee. Then Adamle gazed out through the dusty panes at a freight wagon clattering down the street and at the horses tied to the hitch racks. It seemed a lot of homesteaders were in, and he wondered if the ranchers would try to stir things up. While headquartering at the Red Garter Casino were gunhands hired by the ranchers. From what he'd picked up in the bars Ian MacGregor's cattle company was fanning the flames of discontent among the ranchers. One thing was for certain, Burl Adamle reckoned as his food arrived, the homesteaders were in for hard times.

The beef was tough and stringy, and he took out his pocket knife. There was a brief instant when Adamle glanced out the window at the two men just riding up and leading packhorses. They tied up across the street. The one holding Adamle's attention was the taller man, younger than his companion, and when he turned this way, Adamle felt a start of recognition. *From the way he handles himself,* mused Adamle, *he's been in the army.* He could see the burn marks on the man's face; then the new arrivals were leading their packhorses behind the dry goods store.

Sergeant Burl Adamle had seen duty at a lot of western outposts; so to plumb down exactly where it was he'd seen the man with the scarred face would take some doing. Names kept tripping out of his memory. For some eerie reason he kept returning to Fort Randall and the troopers and officers he'd known there.

"Wait a minute."

It could have been the unexpected arrival earlier this year of Colonel James Ramsey up at Fort Lyon that had brought such a resurgence of that incident down in Texas. That was ages ago, and men will change. But that man he'd seen with the packhorse couldn't have been Lieutenant Chase Donavan.

"No wait a minute about that. Lieutenant Chase Donavan got himself killed seven years ago. Maybe, Adamle, you're getting spooked because Colonel Ramsey is in town."

"I'm tired of waiting . . . waiting. . . ."

"Nobody's shootin' at you, Oberbye."

"I ain't like you, Matt, able to just sit here."

Cy Oberbye swiped off his Stetson and set in on the table. Across from him sat Matt Traxel, and scattered between them on the tabletop were empty whiskey bottles, shot glasses and a deck of cards. Just in back of them Ben Sutthill and Sammy Ronyak were playing a leisurely game of eight ball. Packing the bar here at the Red Garter were a few locals, Anglos. During the day some of the cowhands here attending the meeting being held by the Prairie Cattle Company would drift in and have a couple of drinks or set into a poker game before moving on.

Matt Traxel was also experiencing a desire to get out of Trinidad. Even so, he relished this opportunity to loaf in a town where the law wasn't anxious to run him out. About every other day Traxel had attended meetings over at that Scotsman's big and fancy office. Spread out on the desk and other tables had been a lot of maps. Those new deputies hired by the town of Trinidad had also been there, and they listened to MacGregor detailing just what was to be done once the big cattle ranchers backed up his play. From what Matt Traxel had seen and been told, he was beginning to realize that Ian MacGregor really didn't need the backing of these ranchers, for if something went wrong, MacGregor could lay the blame on these men. Traxel also knew he was an expendable part of MacGregor's plans. But unlike the ranchers with their vast holdings, this place had no hold on him. And those maps had detailed to Traxel that the cattle company run by MacGregor would soon have a million acres of land. But among this acreage were those living on it: homesteaders, nesters, farmers, small ranchers, and the Hispanic plazas. A lot of folks would be uprooted, some against their will, but those who wouldn't sign a quit-claim deed would receive a visit from men like Matt Traxel.

Once this thing got going, and MacGregor became more dependent on him, Traxel meant to strike a new deal. This was going to be the last time Matt Traxel would hire out his gun. The West was changing fast, with the dust along one westbound trail barely clearing before another column of dust rose someplace else. More people out here meant more laws and lawmen. During the days he'd been here, Traxel had watched his companions, and from their remarks he knew they'd never give up this way of life. They hadn't been reading the signs of change. Somehow he envied them, for they would go down with guns blazing and cursing their way into Hades.

He merely nodded as Cy Oberbye reached for his hat and said he wanted some fresh air. As Oberbye shoved through the batwings, Traxel's crooked finger summoned a barmaid with a bottle of whiskey. When he dropped some money into her hand, she threw him a teasing smile before moving away. Refilling his shot glass, Matt Traxel began pondering the future of Cy Oberbye. He'd found out from Ben Sutthill that Cy had gotten into the habit of going to Chinese opium dens, and that if word of this got out, Oberbye would take out old Ben. Maybe the simple thing to do, especially since a few more gunhands he knew had arrived at Trinidad, was to give Oberbye some money and tell him to find work elsewhere. But in the past he could always rely on Cy, be it backing him in a gunfight or doing a simple killing. Men with that quality were hard to find. What would help all of them was to get out and start hammering lead into a sodbuster or two. This had always calmed Traxel's nerves before. He'd lost count of all those he'd killed. Not that it mattered any.

There was one killing that when talked about always provoked smiles from everyone. The four of them, and three others of their bloody craft, had stopped at Cimarron, located just west of Dodge City. They'd been at this trading post on the outskirts of town buying supplies and seeing to their horses, their next stop being farther north at Tribune and one of its banks. Into the trading post had wandered a bony, wizened man clad in ragged clothing, his plaintive attempt to get some wine from the owner bringing an angry retort.

"So you need some wine," muttered Traxel.

"Just a bottle will do," the wino replied hopefully.

"Fetch me the biggest bottle of wine you've got."

"Mister, it's a waste of money—" the bartender began.

"But it's my money." Matt Traxel picked up the large bottle of cheap red wine and, followed by the wino and the other outlaws, headed out back where their horses were tied near the watering tank. Traxel walked on a little farther to the woodpile and set the bottle of wine down on a block of wood. When he swung around, the wino was there eagerly eying what he sought above anything else.

"There's a catch, my friend."

Puzzled eyes peered up at the outlaw. "A . . . a catch?"

"You make a grab to drink from that bottle and I'll gun you down." He laughed softly as the wino stumbled backward. "The bottle's yours, my friend. What you crave most can kill you. Something to think about." He watched as the raggedy wino scurried into the shadow of the trading post, and then Traxel joined the others enjoying some coffee and food.

"A hard choice," said one.

"I'd say no choice," said another.

"Will he do it?"

"I'm saying he will."

"Okay, Traxel, a hundred says he don't."

"I'm willing to wager another hundred," cut in Matt Traxel, "that he goes for the bottle within the hour. Ben, unlimber that watch of yours."

"It's five after three," chortled Ben Sutthill.

"Anytime within the next hour."

"Matt, dammit, I'll take that bet. 'Cause there's no way that wino or anybody else is gonna commit suicide over a bottle of anything."

During the next half hour it became a deadly waiting game, the outlaws seated around and quiet, eying Matt Traxel or trying to see what the wino was doing. During this time alluring sunshine kept glittering off the large bottle of wine upon which the eyes of the outlaws became more and more fixed. For a while the wino had disappeared, and one outlaw whispered the vain hope the man had come to his senses and drifted back into town. Then the wino slunk out from behind the trading post and began working his way along a pole corral. Finally there was only open space to confront him and the prize he craved, and whimpering in his desire to get what he sought, the wino darted forward. Clawing hands wrapped around the large bottle and pulled out the cork. Desperately he raised the heavy bottle as his lips sought the bitter wine. The sudden report of Matt Traxel's six-gun echoed a heartbeat after a leaden slug blew a hole in the wino's head.

"Let's ride" was all that Traxel said, and needed to be said.

Years later, and here at this saloon, Matt Traxel

knew that the vices of men always brought about their downfall. That wino had a choice. So did Cy Oberbye, but opium was a hard habit to break. Was that Scotsman any different with his lust for land? Not the way Matt Traxel saw it.

"Soon it'll be the day of the widow maker."

Chapter Nine

"Yessir, Mr. Donavan, this is the best year I've had in Trinidad."

"I'm glad Jacob and I could make it even better. Hilario Madrid said you treat everyone squarely."

"The way I am, I reckon," said Albee Porter as one of his clerks started locking the front door of his dry goods store. "Seen a lot of trail herds passing through. Got plenty of business from those herding them. But ever since homesteaders have been arrivin' and settling in, business has been steadier."

"I couldn't help noticing," said Jacob Purcell, "that a lot of your customers are Mexicans."

"Guess I've been here so long everyone knows me. Early on, a man had to take what trade he could get. Too bad you boys are heading back instead of staying over. That's a long ride at night. There'll be some special activities happening in town tonight. Mostly put on by the cattlemen. A few dances and such. It could be too that Judge Darcy Halloran will unlimber his sonorous pipes as he belabors the Republicans. And special services will be held at the church."

"Yes, church," Purcell said wistfully. "Back home we never missed Sunday services."

"You'd like our choir, Mr. Purcell."

Chase turned and glanced out the open back door at the late afternoon sun. Jacob's family was staying at his place until they returned. Though he'd promised Raven they would make this a one day trip, there'd been growing in Chase this temptation to look over the town and find out what Trinidad was all about. As Albee Porter had just mentioned, a long ride at night along the river road could be hazardous. Part of Chase's reluctance to stay was that he'd seen a few soldiers idling about town, but the way he looked now, the homespun clothes and marked face, it was a remote possibility that his own mother would recognize him. As a gambler he'd learned to read the odds, at cards or when someone was bluffing, and what he didn't want now was that remote possibility of someone linking him to the past.

With some reluctance he said, "Town's awful crowded. Meaning there'll be no vacant rooms available."

"See those sheds out back, Mr. Donavan?" The store owner beamed. "Got some spare beds in there I've been meaning to sell; blankets and pillows to go with them. Pack your gear in there for tonight. Put your horses in my corrals. No charge, since I want to keep any new customers."

"That is neighborly of you, Mr. Porter."

"Mr. Purcell, staying over will give you an opportunity to attend church services commencin' at seven."

"But we did promise—"

"Jacob, we knuckle in to our wives all the time, no telling what will happen. Mr. Porter, if you'll show us where to stow our pack saddles. . . ."

Long after Jacob Purcell had left to attend church, Chase savored his cigarillo while listening to the haunting Mexican music coming from a distant cantina. The shed they would spend the night in gave off a musky scent, but it was reasonably clean. He sat on a chair by the open doorway and thought about what next year would bring. He could buy some cattle from Hilario Madrid, who'd also mentioned that the stockyards could have some dreg cattle for sale. These were animals that had become sore-footed on those long cattle drives up from Texas and were dropped off at places like Trinidad to be sold cheap. In the morning he could check this out.

"And there's money."

There was enough to see him through the winter and spring. After that he would have to rely on selling hay or whatever crop he put in and any cattle he might own. He could always pick up some extra money at trapping or hooking on with a local rancher. Anything to keep the place he had. Chase figured his chances were better than those coming out from the East in that he knew the country out here and the men living in it, the cowpunchers, ranchers, plainsmen, Indian. But it wouldn't take too many bad breaks to have a man go under.

Back when that salesman had stopped at his place, the one who'd sold him the sewing machine, the man had told of this new cattle company settling here in Trinidad and of the troubles it had caused. From his experience as a cavalry officer, he knew a law was good only if it had a lot of backing out here. Mostly these were just a lot of foolhardy legal words to men accustomed to making their own laws. The store owner, Albee Porter, had confirmed that it was the intention of the Prairie Cattle Company to try and buy out smaller property owners. Another thing that Chase had noticed since riding in today was the presence of men more commonly seen in places like Dodge City or Abilene. This get-together that was taking place in town between the big cattlemen could be bad news for the homesteader. Whenever checking into a new town, gambler Chase Donavan always dropped in for a courtesy visit with the local law. More than once this had bailed him out of a tight corner. A visit now would explain a lot of things. Earlier, he had declined going to supper with Jacob; scratching at his stomach was a vague emptiness.

"Might's well get the lay of this place."

Down in one of the cantinas Sheriff Juan Guiterrez had come across one of those hard-eyed Anglos lashing a barmaid across the face with a pigging string, the short length of rawhide drawing blood. And when Cy Oberbye tore the woman's white blouse, Guiterrez had no choice but to grab the Anglo's arm and spin him away from the woman.

"You damned greaser—" The gunhand backed up to get his bearings, and he grinned tightly when he saw the sheriff's badge. Cy Oberbye had been drinking steadily since early afternoon in an attempt to calm his jangling nerves. What a helluva town where a man couldn't buy some opium. Now this greaser of a sheriff had to show up.

"Easy, *hombre*," said Guiterrez, "there is no need for gunplay. But I insist you leave these people alone."

"You'd better do your insisting with that gun, damn you." Oberbye lashed out and spilled a bottle of whiskey off the bar top as erratic laughter tore out of his mouth. "You don't draw, greaser, I'll kill you anyway."

"And if you draw, *hombre*"—Juan Guiterrez nodded with his eyes—"my deputy will blow your head off." The sheriff smiled thinly, but only with his taut lips. "Now the choice is yours . . . *hombre?*"

94

The gunhand wavered between snaking a look over his shoulder and saying to hell with it and unleathering his six-gun. In Oberbye's eyes was unmasked hatred for the greaser with the badge. He took another backward step, letting his head turn first to the right and then left at those backed up against the walls. There wasn't a friendly eye in the whole damned cantina for the Anglo.

"I'm waiting . . . *hombre*. . . ."

The sheriff's calm manner unnerved Oberbye, but what really made up the gunhand's mind was Deputy Sheriff Tafoya drawing the hammer back on the Greener from where he stood framed in an open window, that rasping click finally making Oberbye comprehend he was in alien territory.

"Damn you greasers," the gunhand said. "I . . . I was just funning around with that woman. . . ."

Sheriff Guiterrez said, "I suggest you vamoose, pronto."

"I'll see you again, Sheriff . . . when the odds are more even."

Guiterrez stepped toward the bar and replied, "I do not like being threatened in my town, *hombre*. So I'm asking you to leave. You have until tomorrow at sundown. *Adios* until then, *hombre*.

Deputy Tafoya kept his shotgun at the ready until the hardcase came out of the cantina and headed up the street. In the cantina Tafoya glanced briefly at the woman pressing a wet cloth to her bleeding face. "I know her, one of Pedro Juarez's daughters." He moved to stand by Guiterrez. "Lucky we paired up tonight."

"Not so lucky for her."

"After you went to supper, Juan, more gunmen rode in."

They went outside and stood in the dark street. Guiterrez stared eastward at the back of the Colorado

Hotel towering over the other buildings. He would be glad when the ranchers left town. Most of the trouble lately had been caused by men working for MacGregor and his cattle company. Just the other day he'd broken up a fight between a homesteader and one of those gunhands. The homesteader hadn't been carrying a weapon, and Guiterrez knew that if he hadn't shown up the hardcase would have pulled out his gun. The presence of these intruders in Trinidad had served to temper relations between the Anglos and his own people. This would all change when Ian MacGregor started buying land again.

"I tell you . . . we don't have the best of jobs. We should be out patrolling around the county. Instead we dare not leave town," the sheriff said.

"These new deputies . . . I *pensamiento —* "

"Those three pigs only serve MacGregor," Guiterrez said bitterly. "We'll split up. If there's trouble . . . it'll be downtown. And remember, Tafoya, if a gunfighter is involved, look for either me or Rodriques or Valdez."

"Si, but let's pray nothing happens tonight."

After the deputy found a side street, Sheriff Guiterrez checked out the remaining cantinas before trudging down a gravely path passing by a livery stable. It was late, by his estimate going on midnight. Before all of these hard-eyed men had come to Trinidad, evenings would find Juan Guiterrez at his adobe home. They would retire early, and if he wasn't too tired, he would make love to his wife. It had been a good life.

"No siento lo quie he hecho." I have no regrets for what I've done.

Long before Sheriff Juan Guiterrez reached Main Street he heard music, most of it Hispanic, some hoe-down, but all of these bands going at it to fetch more customers into the saloons and dance halls. He came onto the street at its western end, this just a widening of the road going out to link with the Santa Fe Trail. He could use a drink, more to drive out the night chill than for any craving of it, and would get some tequila when his tour of duty was over. Maybe it was that encounter with the hardcase, or just plain nerves, that held Guiterrez in the deeper shadows along the front of the building. Something didn't seem right.

Though the Prairie Cattle Company had paid for the shindig going on at the Colorado Hotel, it seemed to Guiterrez that all of Trinidad was out tonight, for even at this late hour some of the trading posts were still open and doing some business. A woman's scream ripped out of a saloon window, followed by laughter, causing Guiterrez to swear.

"Damned whores . . . just like some *maldito* alley cats. . . ."

"Buenos noches."

Guiterrez nodded at a merchant named Harper strolling past. The man was on the city council, was one of those who'd voted against putting on more deputies. Men like Harper wanted all the protection they could get but were too tightfisted to pay for it, or for that matter, hated to spend more money to improve the streets. He'd seen it before, someone coming in here to start a business, probably make a good return on his investment before selling out and moving on. Not a dime of that money sucked out of the townspeople would ever benefit Trinidad. Most of these Anglos were like that, whereas the Mexicans had no choice but to stay and weather out the bad years which often struck a place like this.

Sheriff Juan Guiterrez's scowl pushed away some of his unexplained nervousness as his boots sounded on the boardwalk. This end of Main Street had more shadow clinging to it and had no street lamps. Coming to a side street, he paused to flick a glance down it.

After three cowpokes rode by, Guiterrez crossed over and checked out a small saloon owned by a Welshman name Carradine. This evening Guiterrez had on a plain leather coat. His badge lay underneath pinned to his woolen shirt. He nodded at Carradine, a tall, reedy man wearing a derby.

"Care for a drink, Juan?"

"Not tonight. The town hasn't been this lively in a long time."

"Celebrations being kind'a sparse around here . . . a lot of folks welcome the opportunity to bolster their spirits."

"All your customers are locals."

"Strangers shy away when they see that dart board and the two poker tables; my place is too small for their gambling tastes."

"You have seen them around town, these gunmen?"

"They're easy to spot, Sheriff."

"There was one I chased out of Torrez's place . . . a sandy-haired man with a drooping lip. He's packing a Starr .44."

"Hasn't been in here tonight. Caused a ruckus?"

"Beat up a woman."

Guiterrez had been collecting the names of these gunmen, and then telegraphing out to see if any of them were wanted by the law, only to have one of the clerks working at the telegraph office pay a visit to the Prairie Cattle Company. Shortly afterward Ian MacGregor had dropped over to the jail to inform the sheriff of Las Animas County he was overstepping his authority.

"Caramba!" Guiterrez retorted. "Consorting with gunmen means you're no better than a whoremaster."

Now, almost a month later, Juan Guiterrez felt threatened as into Trinidad drifted more hard-eyed men. Some of them had merely used the town as a rendezvous point before riding out to one or another of the bigger ranches. They'd been hired to take out after the homesteaders. On his trips around the county Guiterrez had come across many a grave site. There'd be a lot more, compliments of a disease called lead poisoning.

Out in the street he found the wind had picked up to beat against the shingled roofs and moan through the gaps between buildings. But music still shrilled out of the saloons as Guiterrez checked out the locked doors of business places while easing along the wide street. This block had a few street lights, and when he got to the next intersection, a man called out, "Hey, Sheriff, there's trouble over here!"

Down on a side street passing to the southeast Guiterrez could hear the sharp crack of a man's fist hitting bone, and he hurried that way. He passed a long shed, then swung in to where a man packing a handgun was measuring a nester to hit the man again. The nester reeled back into the side of his wagon from the force of another blow, and he grabbed the sideboards to keep from falling.

"Enough!" Guiterrez yelled.

The gunman shifted sideways and shaped a crooked grin for the sheriff. "This damned fool was asking for it. And I aim to keep hammering away until I scramble what brains he's got left. Unless . . . Guiterrez, you plan to stop me?"

"I know you? You're one of those hired on by Ian MacGregor."

"That a fact," snarled the gunman as he swung back and slammed his fist into the nester's ribcage.

"I said enough!" said the sheriff. And when the gunman turned back to face him, Juan Guiterrez knew there'd be gunplay. He accepted it, calmly, angrily, though he was no great shakes with a six-gun. "I'm asking you to hand over your weapon."

"Greaser, you can go to hell." The gunhand tensed, then smiled as a gun sounded and the nester stiffened in shock, and as he began falling, that same gun hammered again, once more.

Sheriff Juan Guiterrez took two slugs in the back . . . the pain coming now . . . the harsh realization he'd walked into a trap. He tried to draw his own weapon, tried and failed as his legs began buckling. He dropped to his knees as the man who'd ambushed him came around the nester's wagon, and then Guiterrez knew it was the gunman he'd encountered in the cantina. He saw the barrel of the six-gun swinging to level on his chest.

"Drop it!" someone spat out.

Cy Oberbye jerked his eyes away from the sheriff to the shadowy form of a man just clearing the shed. "Let's take him," Oberbye told the other hardcase. As Oberbye's finger tightened on the trigger, a leaden slug ripped into his throat, and he fired into the ground. Dead legs held the gunman up for a brief moment before he fell heavily by Guiterrez.

In the uncertain light glowing from Main Street the other gunhand wasn't certain if he'd scored a hit at the intruder still striding toward him. He fired again, wildly. Something snagged into his shoulder . . . he felt himself spinning sideways . . . a second slug drove the air out of his shattered lungs . . . and he whimpered in surprise. When he brought up a gloved hand to wipe the moisture away from his mouth, it came to the gunman that what stained his glove was his own blood. Then a final bullet severed his spine to chase the spark of life out of his disbelieving eyes.

Chase Donavan had been idling just outside of a saloon when his eyes landed upon the sheriff making his nightly rounds. Chase had also heard someone call out to the sheriff, with curiosity bringing Chase back along that side street. He got there just as one of the gunmen hammered another fist at the nester. Then a gun began barking off to Chase's left. What happened next was just reflex action on Chase Donavan's part. What probably saved him was that he could see better at night than most men.

By the time Chase leathered his gun others were arriving, and someone called out that it was the tall man with the scarred face who'd gone to the aid of the sheriff. But Chase ignored all of this as he knelt before Juan Guiterrez and said softly, "How bad is it, Sheriff?"

"In the back . . . but I still live. *Señor . . . por favor . . . gracias.*"

Chase wrapped an arm around Guiterrez's chest and lowered him to the ground so that he lay on his stomach. "I need some help to get him to a doctor. What about that sodbuster?"

"He's dead señor," a bystander replied.

"Too bad."

"Can I have your name?"

He looked at the man who'd asked, then around at those standing there and just coming in. "My name isn't important. Tend to your sheriff first."

"Quickly . . . you . . . and you . . . we must take Guiterrez to Doc Pritchard's."

Then another man inquired as to Donavan's identity, and Chase turned and looked at a Mexican wearing a deputy sheriff's badge. "I'm new here abouts . . . but my name's Donavan. I'm homesteading just north of here."

"Señor Donavan . . . I'm Juan Tofoya. This man over here gave us some trouble tonight. Do you know him?"

"Nope."

"Or the other one?"

"He'll rest just as easy on boot hill, Tafoya."

"*Si* . . . the dead embrace all. I only pray that Sheriff Guiterrez doesn't wind up there. You're homesteading up north?"

"If you need any references, Tafoya, just drop in and see Hilario Madrid."

"*Muchas gracias,* Señor Donavan, but I feel that won't be necessary."

The darkness hid Chase moving back toward Main Street. Pausing under a street lamp, he found that his hands were trembling, and he smiled wryly. By now he should know better than to involve himself in the affairs of others. But he certainly didn't expect to be gunning it out with those ambushers.

"I can't believe it's . . . you. . . ."

He stiffened and stepped away from the haloing light while wheeling around to find himself staring at a soldier.

"You've changed—those marks on your face and all—but no question now that you're Lieutenant Chase Donavan. . . ."

His wary eyes went to the bold yellow sergeant strips adorning each blue sleeve. The beard was tinged with gray, though the face was of a man in his middle thirties. There was no stir of recognition in Chase for this soldier; but it was all too clear that the man knew him, and within Chase Donavan there came a forbidding fear.

"Sir, those Coyoteros reported that you'd been killed. So as far as the army was concerned its business with you was over. Yes, I reckon you wouldn't remember me. Lieutenant Donavan, I was a corporal then—"

"A corporal? At . . . Fort Randall?"

"Yessir. Corporal Burl Adamle. It was me, sir, that got you out of that stockade. Got you outside the main gates . . . where a horse was waiting . . . and you, sir, you rode off. And the way those Coyoteros told it, sir, it was lightning that done you in."

"Sergeant Adamle," he said hesitantly, "let's say that lightning storm left its calling card. Reckon I am Donavan." He extended his hand, which was clasped by the sergeant. "Reckon I owe you my life too, Adamle."

"What say we wet our whistles at that bar, sir."

"After all of what's happened tonight, Sergeant, I could use one or two. You stationed hereabouts?" They moved down the street, swung into a saloon and found a back table.

"Up at Fort Lyons."

"North along the Arkansas River."

"A real hellhole. Chiefly because of our commanding officer."

"The army's no Sunday School, Adamle."

"I knew—and others did too—that you didn't kill Sergeant Riddell. I know for a fact he was murdered by Colonel Ramsey. Tried to speak up back then, sir, but it wouldn't have made no difference, as Ramsey had filed charges against you."

"I know how the system works. Lost track of Ramsey some time back, Adamle. Getting so now it doesn't make much difference anymore."

"It's downright eerie how things work out, sir. After all these years me running into you. Then to have Colonel James Ramsey become the new commander up at Fort Lyons."

A bleak look came into Chase's eyes, and he muttered, "Ramsey's there?"

"He is, sir, damn his black soul."

A barmaid slid a bottle onto their table along with a couple of shot glasses, and Chase found himself handing the woman a silver dollar. As Adamle filled their glasses, Chase stared at a distant point on the wall, his mind reeling over what he'd just been told.

"And wouldn't you know it, sir, I spotted Colonel Ramsey coming in on the stage this morning."

"He's here . . . in Trinidad . . . ?"

"He was. Ramsey could have left by now."

"James . . . Ramsey," Chase intoned. "All the misery he's caused me. Now he's here. The question is, Adamle, what now?"

"I don't understand, Lo'tenant—"

"Is he worth killing?"

Chapter Ten

"The land ought to tell you, Johnson, it was never meant to be plowed. Look at them furrows . . . no moisture in that rocky ground."

"I intend to build an irrigation ditch up from the creek."

An hour ago Jake Leach and the other two deputies had left the Purgatoire River and ridden along this creek until they came across this homestead. Armed with some quit-claim deeds and money given to them by the Prairie Cattle Company, they hoped to persuade Johnson and others like him to sell out.

Jake Leach fixed his eyes upon the sodhouse built into the side of a low hill and the woman staring out through the open door. He could see the despair etched on her thin face. He knew Johnson's wife would sell out in a minute, and then make tracks back east. The small pole corral was shared by an ox and a gelding. Cottonwoods held back the full force of the autumn wind, the yellow leaves they were shedding flung aimlessly about. One gaunt rooster jumped down from the roof of the outhouse and tookout after a hen, and Leach's bronc snorted nervously.

He looked back at the homesteader while trying to keep from losing his temper. Their orders from Ian

MacGregor were to leave peaceably if the landowner wouldn't sell. But right about now Leach wanted to unlimber his six-gun and shed some blood. He wasn't the patient kind; neither were Wyman and Pierce.

"Johnson, I'll say it for the last time. I'm offering you a hundred dollars for this place."

"It cost me far more'n that to journey out here, Mr. Leach. I figure on being here a long time. Would offer you some coffee but we're plumb out."

"You're a plague upon the land, Johnson," the gunman retorted.

They rode back along the creek, and then drew up beyond where it bent to the northwest. Leach swung down by a cottonwood as Wyman pulled a small flask out of his coat pocket and drank some whiskey.

"How's about passing it over," said Pierce.

"Why don't you buy your own corn liquor once in a while."

"It's cheaper spongin' off'n you."

"Go to hell."

"Lay off that stuff," said Jake Leach, as he nailed a quit-claim deed to the tree; using a black crayon he'd marked the piece of paper with a large X. "That should take care of the Johnsons."

Back in the saddle, he went ahead to bring the others in a circular course around the homesteader's buildings and farther along the creek. From the map given him by the cattle company, he knew others had taken up homesteads along this creek. It was still morning, and it would be a long day for the three deputies, and so would the days to follow.

"We're gonna have to be more persuasive," he said.

"A little hot lead can make up a man's mind in a hurry."

"That's what Traxel and his bunch are gettin' paid to do."

"Maybe if you shaved that mangy beard off, Jake—"

"Wyman, the first day out and already I'm getting tired of your smart mouth. You should talk . . . a coon could hide out in that long hair of yours and you'd never notice."

The other deputy, Pierce, chuckled to himself. Before hiring on with the cattle company their specialty had been holding up stagecoaches down in the Panhandle and varying parts of Texas. It was from others of their craft they'd heard about this setup being offered by the cattle company. In a way it was the first honest work they'd ever done. Though any day he expected a Texas Ranger to find them. If that happened, it would be a bloody showdown.

Far ahead a small column of smoke trickled over an elevation, and Pierce muttered, "This time maybe me and Wyman better do the talking, Jake."

"From all the territory we've got to cover," retorted Jake Leach, "it won't be long before all of us are talked out."

"I still say a gun speaks better than words," Wyman insisted.

"Maybe so, Wyman, but you ain't ramrodding this operation."

"What if one of these nesters makes a grab for his rifle?"

"Shoot to kill, I figure."

The sudden demise of Cy Oberbye didn't cause the other gunmen any concern. Along with a hard-eyed drifter out of Arkansas, Matt Traxel had hired on four others. These were killers known to Traxel. A day after the sheriff had been gunned down, orders had come from the Prairie Cattle Company to head out of Trinidad, as a deal had been struck with the cattle barons.

107

This meant these men would look the other way when Traxel and his bunch rode across their land in search of homesteaders.

One thing that puzzled Matt Traxel as he rode away from the lowering sun was how Cy Oberbye and that other gunhand had been done in by a sodbuster. The name Chase Donavan meant nothing to Traxel. But according to witnesses Oberbye had his handgun out when Donavan showed up. It could have been that both of the gunmen were drunk, or that Oberbye had found himself some opium.

"A man chooses his own poison," Traxel muttered.

"What's that, Matt?"

"Just mulling things over, Ben."

"Is this what we're looking for?" Ronyak asked.

The gunmen had been riding strung out along a creek. Taking the point was Sammy Ronyak as they followed the trail left by the trio of deputies. Now the others came up to Ronyak sitting his horse under a cottonwood. He nodded at a piece of paper tacked to the tree and grinned back at Matt Traxel.

"What we're looking for, Sammy," Traxel replied.

Ben Sutthill, unsheathing his rifle, said, "It still isn't clear to me if we're to leave any witnesses."

"MacGregor said not to harm women and children," Traxel told them. "But we'll kill anyone bringing a weapon against us. Head out now."

Matt Traxel waited until his men had split into two bunches, those with Sammy Ronyak splashing across the creek and vanishing beyond thick underbrush, Sutthill taking the rest around to the east to circle in toward the homestead. As Traxel sat there waiting for his men to get into position, he pondered over what was to come in the days ahead. All it would take was one or two homesteaders holding out against him to make others take a like stand. That homesteader who'd

108

gunned down Cy Oberbye was one example, and by now Chase Donavan's neighbors were looking to the man for leadership. He had argued with Ian MacGregor about taking out Donavan first, as well as those Hispanics entrenched along the Purgatoire. But the Scotsman had insisted they clean out the points of less resistance first. This would serve to warn those Hispanics that it was time to sell out and move on.

"You're wrong, MacGregor,"—the gunfighter knew, as he spurred around the cottonwood—"even about having your so-called guardians of the law—these deputies—palaver with these scum."

The black gelding upon seeing the buildings unfolding beyond a bend in the creek whickered a greeting to the horse standing in the corral. Loping on in, Traxel saw sunlight reflect off a rifle held by one of his men hidden on the far side of the creek.

The homesteader stopped working on a hand scythe and picked up an old muzzle-loader. From there he moved closer to the corral and steadied the long barrel of his weapon on a pole and called out, "Hold it right there, mister!"

The gunman slowed his horse to a walk but kept coming in until he reached the small patch of barren yard around the buildings, where Traxel drew up and folded his arms over the saddle horn. Deliberately he'd ridden in closer to be within six-gun range. How many others were there? Those deputies should have written down the name of the sodbuster also, and displeasure rippled across Traxel's face, for he could be facing any number of hidden guns.

Brazenly he said, "Someone just made you an offer to sell out."

"That's right, stranger. Not that it's any of your business. Just what is it you want?"

"You're a fool." Carefully the gunman lifted his left

hand and adjusted the brimmed Stetson.

At the heavy report of a rifle the homesteader was driven against the corral by a slug ripping into his back. Before the echoing sound of the rifle had died away, Traxel swung down and unleathered his handgun as he ran over to the sodhouse. He strode onto the porch and leveled his gun at the open doorway.

"Anybody in there?" He heard a scuffling noise and triggered a bullet into the house.

"No . . . please. . . ." a woman cried out.

"Come out where I can see you!" Traxel stepped against the wall, and when the woman emerged, he grabbed her arm and threw her forward off the porch; then the gunman broke inside. He searched the two rooms and went outside and stared at the woman still sprawled on the ground. Sobs racked her body as one hand groped blindly toward the dead form of her husband stretched out by the corral. "You had your chance to clear out."

As his men rode in, Matt Traxel moved up to the corral. The horse reared at his presence and broke, running behind the ox standing there impassively as it looked at the intruder. It took two slugs from Traxel's gun to kill the ox, and then he looked at Ben Sutthill swinging down while reloading.

"Soft work," laughed Sutthill.

"What about the woman?"

Traxel looked at the hardcase from Arkansas, then at the others sitting their saddles alongside, and he said, "I left that horse for her."

"Been a spell, Matt, since I've had a woman."

"Me too," piped up another.

"Have your fun with her, then. But she's not to be killed. I'll give you boys a half hour to have your way with her. Come on, Ben, Sammy."

They were all set to camp out along the creek when weapons began cutting loose in the far distance. Twilight was just hanging its darkening fingers over rimrock, and it had been Matt Traxel's idea to make camp instead of seeking out Jake Leach and his cohorts. They were still saddlebound, so a curt word from Traxel brought them in a ragged column along the creek. "I figure Jake Leach must have said some unkind words."

"Or mouthed something stupid. He's no great shakes at poker either," one of the men added.

"Maybe we'll get lucky and Leach'll get gunned down."

Traxel rode through the underbrush first, with the other riders following the gunman away from the creek and back onto the prairie. All the while the heavy sound of rifles reverberated toward them, along with the softer crackling of six-guns.

"There's chimney smoke," one rider pointed out.

"Okay," said Traxel, "sounds like Leach has taken on more than he can handle. Those buildings are just beyond that ridgeline and maybe a piece up from the creek. Ben, head west around that ridge and come in easy. Me and the others'll sidle along the creek. No sense waiting for any signal; just open up when you get there."

"What if there's women and children down there?" Sammy asked.

The glance Traxel had for Sammy Ronyak was filled with malice, the gunman saying flatly, "No survivors this time. Then we set fire to the buildings."

"No more pussyfooting around," commented Sutthill with a smirking grin. "Suits me, Matt."

In less than a half hour Matt Traxel had brought his men cautiously along the creek bank, with their horses throwing up clods of mud. Where they rode, the outlaws could just see above the high wall of the tapering bank and the fenceline running along it. A few jays took off screeching at their passing. They could make out in the vague light the half-finished walls of a barn, some sheds and a log house. Off to their right and firing from a pile of logs were Leach and his men. Traxel held up a restraining arm.

"What now?" one of the gunmen asked anxiously.

"We count their weapons."

"Never heard of such a thing."

"Learned it from the Comanche," muttered Traxel. After a while he knew from the muzzle flashes at least two homesteaders were firing from the house, two more by the barn, and another in the nearby shed. "I figure old Ben is doing the same thing. But we'll hold here until Sutthill opens up. Then we'll have these damned fools in a crossfire. For now lets find a gap in this fence or make one."

At a walk the gunmen brought their horses up the bank and searching along the fenceline until Schmidt, a lanky outlaw from Wyoming, whispered back that he'd found a gate, and he opened it to the slight creaking of barbed wire.

"We'll leave our horses here and go in on foot," Traxel told them. Now he smiled when Sutthill and the others began hammering slugs at the buildings. One of those defending the homestead cried out in pain, but from counting the weapons being fired Traxel knew the man was still dangerous.

"Spread out and we'll move in. Schmidt, Arkansas, concentrate your fire on that barn. But hold your fire until you get a good target. Shooting at shadows kills damned few men."

The presence of the gunmen brought Jake Leach and his men away from the log pile. One of the homesteaders went down, then another under the relentless fire of the gunmen. Shortly thereafter a woman called out from the house that her husband was sorely wounded, and a white piece of tablecloth began fluttering from a shattered window. Quickly the intruders came in to wrest weapons away from the survivors.

"Clean out that house," Traxel said harshly, "I want everyone out here . . . under moonlight where I can eyeball them."

Only when the homesteaders were clustered together by a shed wall did Matt Traxel realize they'd encountered a man named Robison and his four sons, this according to Jake Leach.

"Didn't give me a chance to get done with my spiel, Traxel, a-fore they was ordering us off at gunpoint. Had no choice then but to try and take them out."

Two of the homesteader's sons held their father upright, and in the man's eyes blazed a bitter hatred. Robison spat out, "Sell out to you murderers? Never!"

"Bold words for a man in your position, Robison."

"Who are you?"

"Makes no matter who I am." Matt Traxel still had a grip on his handgun, though it hung down at his side. He smiled at Robison's wife, but the smile never reached his eyes. "Nice place you folks got here. Too bad about that."

In one swift motion Traxel raised his gun and shot the woman in the stomach; then the other gunmen were hammering away at their victims. No sooner had the sound of gunfire died away, than Traxel ordered his men to drag the bodies into the house and set fire to it and the other buildings as well. As he stood there watching his orders being carried out, Traxel was studying Jake Leach, knowing the man was ill-suited for the job he was supposed to be doing.

"Dammit, Leach, this isn't going to work out."

"This is the first day out Traxel. Once we get the hang of it, things'll go easier. These damnfool sodbusters were just itching for a fight when we rode in. My pa used to be a circuit rider . . . a sort of halfhearted sky pilot. Learned about the Bible from Pa, which is one reason I pack the good book in my possibles."

"Change your speech—sermonize if you've a mind to, Leach—but here's the way it'll be from now on." He glanced at the flames beginning to consume the buildings. "I'll fill you in when we make camp, as I'm saddlesore and damned hungry. By the way, Leach, you've got some maps. Just where does this homesteader live who gunned down Oberbye?"

"From what I gather, up along the Purgatoire. Why?"

"Could be we'll head up thataway before long."

"Hell, Traxel, this job of ours'll take weeks or months before we see all these sodbusters. Besides, MacGregor told us we're to clean out one section before heading into another."

"We're out here and MacGregor's back in Trinidad."

"I don't know. . . ."

"We'll talk on it."

"This fire is going to attract a lot of attention."

"It better," responded Matt Traxel. "I hope it scares out a lot of these sodbusters. Up yonder seems a good spot to pitch our camp, under them elm trees. Men, a good day's work. Killing a man always whets my appetite an' makes whiskey taste better." With a bold smile for his companions, Matt Traxel turned and headed for the fenceline, seeking his horse.

Chapter Eleven

Long after the others had gone to bed Chase Donavan stood on a knoll fronting onto the river. Southeasterly a column of reddish smoke tinged the night sky, which to Chase and others living along the river meant another homestead was going up in the flames. Along with razing homesteads, the marauders were killing innocent people. More than once he'd seen the wagons of those leaving the territory trekking northward on the river road.

Bitterly he'd said, "These are the lucky ones."

In shattered fragments there'd drifted up the Purgatoire the grim news of how the cattle barons had unleashed their hired guns. Up to now these men had raided farther south; but they were coming close to Trinidad, and it wouldn't be too much longer, Chase figured, before some unwelcome visitors would be riding in. It was no secret that the Prairie Cattle Company was working hand in glove with the ranchers. He'd heard of how deputy sheriffs hired by the county of Las Animas were acting as agents for Ian MacGregor. Another matter for concern was that more gunmen had drifted into Trinidad, this adding to the tension between the Anglos and the Hispanics. The strong hand of Sheriff Juan Guiterrez was no longer there to keep the peace, although Guiterrez was recovering from his wounds. Lastly, and more worrisome to Chase, the army seemed reluctant about protecting the homesteaders.

"I could not sleep either."

He glanced over his shoulder at Raven striding up, and a smile creased his face. The overcast sky seemed to press down upon them, the distant glow coming from the receding flames seeming to be a part of the dark clouds. Wrapped around Raven's upper body was an Indian blanket, her dark hair fanning out on it, the worry in her eyes for her husband.

"Are you thinking of that soldier again, Colonel Ramsey?"

"I shouldn't have told you about him."

"In a way, Chase, he gave you to me."

He pondered over this, but mostly about his running into Sergeant Burl Adamle back at Trinidad. Chase had gone looking for James Ramsey, only to learn the colonel had left for Fort Lyon. That day he would have forced the man who'd framed him into a showdown, and damn to what happened afterward. Reflecting on it ever since coming back here, he began to realize that other things had taken the place of his driving hatred for James Ramsey. Chiefly among them were Raven and the boy Jesse, then the new life he was building out here. He could still go up to Fort Lyon and force Colonel Ramsey into confessing he had killed that army sergeant back in Texas. Bitterness still had a strong hold on Chase, a driving need for revenge, but staring at Raven now in the dimness of night, there rose in Chase the knowledge he could stand to loose everything by one rash act.

"Yes," he said grudgingly. "But it was a shock finding out that Ramsey is up at Fort Lyon. When I heard he'd left Trinidad, I had it in mind to follow him up there. Don't know what held me back, Raven. Don't know but one day that's where I'll head."

"I feel the same way about the man who gave me my son. Somehow . . . somehow Micha Colder has become less of a threat . . . now that we have come together, my husband. Yes, Chase, there is still this hatred." She stretched out a lissome arm and touched his cheek. "But you are my life now. Forever, I hope. Perhaps my hatred for Micha Colder will never go away, but because of you it is something I can push aside."

He swept an arm around his wife, to say huskily, "I hope and pray that someday I can be as strong as you. As forgiving." Their lips came together in a lingering kiss.

Then Raven reached for his hand while staring across the river. "At least nothing has happened to us yet. But when Hilario Madrid and his friends come down, I sense unease among them. Will these ranchers force them off their lands?"

"Greed can twist a man's mind," Chase said solemnly. "Another thing, Raven, I've wanted to talk about Jesse going to school, over at Trinidad."

"How can he go there?"

"There's some over at Trinidad who'll take Jesse in during the school months. I want . . . our son to get an education. To make something of himself."

"Jesse has never been away from my side. I don't know. . . ."

"No sense beating around the bush about this," Chase said as they began moving toward the house. "It won't be too much longer before we'll be asked to sell out. Which I have no intention of doing. Neither do Hilario and the others. Or Jacob for that matter. Instead of Jesse going it alone down at that school in Trinidad . . . well, you should be there with him."

"But . . . my place is with you."

"Reckon it is, Raven. It sure makes me feel good having you around. But until this trouble is over, I'd feel a sight better with you and Jesse together in Trinidad. I'll . . . be there whenever I can."

"I know you speak wisdom, Chase. But my heart breaks at the thought of leaving you . . . even for a short while."

"It isn't just me that wants this. Jacob and his wife figure on boarding their yonkers over at Trinidad too for the school year. So at least Jesse'll have someone there he knows."

"I'll sleep on this." She went ahead of Chase into the living room and stepped to the table to turn the wick up on the coal oil lamp. Turning to him, Raven let her eyes sweep tenderly over his face. "What you are saying is that there could be gunplay out here . . . that we could be burned out too."

"Could be. Heard that some folks from Trinidad have sent a delegation up to Fort Lyon. They want the army to station some troops in their town, along with urging the army to send out more patrols to try and hunt down those burning out the homesteaders. Trouble is, commanding up at Fort Lyon is the man who framed me."

"For what reason was the colonel at Trinidad?"

"That was the same question Sergeant Adamle and I tossed around. Strange that Ramsey would be there at the same time those ranchers were in Trinidad holding a powwow." He eased onto a chair as Raven brought the coffeepot over and filled two cups.

"Doesn't the army have . . . how do you say it . . . ?"

"Jurisdiction over this territory? It does. It can declare martial law . . . do whatever it pleases—be it against Indians or anybody else—to keep things under control."

"The coffee isn't very warm."

"Nope, it isn't." Smiling languidly, he reached out a hand and touched her hair, and then by unspoken accord they rose together. With a graceful movement she turned out the lamp and followed her husband into their bedroom.

Later, under the downy covering, they sought solace in each other's arms, and after a while the world outside their homestead faded away.

"*Si*, Hilario Madrid told me about you. And such a beautiful wife you have, Señor Donavan."

"She's that, Señor Sanchez. Your house . . . your *casa* is very nice."

"And enough room for your wife and son."

"The boy needs an education, along with some new clothes. What do you think of that, Jesse?"

Scowling, Jesse Keepseagle said, "I do not like it here."

"Like it or not, son, you'll be going to school. Guess you'll need a haircut too." Chase, with the help of their Mexican host, removed the luggage from the wagon and carried it into the house.

Later that afternoon a pensive Chase Donavan drove away from the house. His inquiries at the sheriff's office brought him down a dusty lane and to the home of Juan Guiterrez. He needed information that only someone who'd lived here a long time could give, but upon stepping onto the front porch of the adobe house, he was greeted with suspicious eyes by a slender woman. Only when Chase told her his name did a

119

smile bring the light of gladness into her eyes.

"So you are the man who saved my husband's life?" she said. Stepping out onto the porch, she embraced Chase. *"Con mucho gusto* I welcome you to our home."

"How is Juan?"

"It goes slowly."

Duffing his hat, he followed her through the living room and down a wide corridor. She gestured to a door, and Chase nodded his thanks and passed through it to find Juan Guiterrez gazing at him from a wide metal-frame bed.

"Si . . . you are the one," Guiterrez said simply while reaching out a hand, which Chase shook warmly. "Pull up a chair and tell me just what it is you want, Señor Donavan."

Chase dragged over a chair and sat down, then he dropped his hat on the floor and said, "Just some answers to a few questions, Juan. But first, how are you feeling?"

"Getting stronger every day. But not so anxious to pin on my badge."

"Being a lawman in these parts can be a thankless job."

"Did you ever wear a badge?"

"Never was that unlucky." Chase smiled.

"Then never wear one. Those who hire you expect miracles. Those you arrest swear vengeance. And those you protect think you aren't doing your job. A vicious circle, Señor Donavan."

"The name's Chase."

"So be it. One thing is puzzling me, Chase. How is it that a homesteader can face up to known gunmen?"

"The truth?"

"As much as you want to tell me."

"Among other things I was a gambler."

120

"The way you carry yourself . . . perhaps you were a *soldado* . . . but no matter. My old *compadre* Hilario Madrid swears by you and of how you came to be known as El Condor." Guiterrez's eyes slid to that part of Chase's face marked by his encounter with lightning. "Ill fortune for Trinidad began when Ian MacGregor arrived here. He has, shall we say, greased the palms of our county authorities; chief among these betrayers is Judge Halloran."

"For what purpose?"

"A good question, since MacGregor's cattle company has title to thousands of acres of ranchland. But in order to raise a lot of cattle one needs plenty of water. This is where the homesteaders have been settling. They come in blindly, almost, drawn to the land along creeks and waterholes. There they plow up virgin prairie in the vain hope of growing crops. Vainly, Chase, because in the hot days of summer a lot of waterways shrivel up and die. So it seems out here that only cattle can survive."

"The ranchers consider them, or us, interlopers, I guess," said Chase. "But the Homestead Act makes it legal for anyone to stake out a claim to some land."

"Of course. Everyone knows this. But out here it is the gun that decides final ownership."

"Seems it's always been that way in these parts. And I can't blame a rancher for wanting to protect what it took him years to build up. But when it comes to murder, Juan, that's a new deal of the cards."

"I agree, wholeheartedly. But what MacGregor and the cattle barons have is power and the means to use it. They will stop at nothing to achieve their bloody aims. Which is why, Chase, I fear for those of my people living on their small plazas. They harm no one . . . through hard work they make their small crops flourish

. . . but they are peace loving people. Some of them, I've heard, have already been asked to sell out. This they do not *comprender.*"

"The key to stopping this, as you know, Juan, is the U.S. Army."

"So, we finally get around to Colonel Ramsey. I heard you were asking about him . . . on the day this happened to me. . . ."

"I was. But he'd left town."

Guiterrez picked up a glass and sipped water from it. "I also heard that you encountered an enlisted man. This I learned because Sergeant Adamle has been seeing an Hispanic woman. Does this mean you knew the sergeant from before?"

"That's part of it," Chase admitted.

"I felt as much. This man Ramsey troubles me . . . troubles me deeply. Something doesn't feel right about the man. It is terrible, I suppose, I say this about the one man who has military jurisdiction over this part of Colorado. But the question you've come to ask, Señor Donavan, is what was Colonel James Ramsey doing here on the day I was shot down. All I can say is that Ramsey came to see Ian MacGregor."

"I believe we know the reason why."

"Perhaps we do, Chase. But proving that the colonel has sold out to MacGregor and those cattle barons is another matter."

"This would explain why the army is reluctant to station some troops here, Juan. And why the army isn't out after those burning out the homesteaders and committing murder."

"Probably," said Guiterrez. "Which brings us back to you, Señor Donavan. I feel that you knew Ramsey from before."

At last Chase knew he'd come to a fork in the trail,

one that by denying any past connection to James Ramsey would see his past remain hidden, the other fork a dagger that could see him being turned over to the army. During this brief time with Juan Guiterrez he'd come to respect the man and his honesty. But if he narrated in untarnished words to Guiterrez what had happened back in Texas, would the man believe him? In him was this tug of war, that sense of caution he'd ingrained in himself ever since fleeing from Fort Randall telling Chase to remain silent. But fighting to be heard were Raven . . . and Jesse . . . and just perhaps those recently murdered by these gunmen.

"Once I could see out of both eyes, Juan." Chase stood up and turned to look out a window at the distant hulk of the Rockies to the northwest. His gaze held on a place he'd once ventured into for a brief time. "Once I was a cavalry officer. My last duty station was down in Texas."

"And Colonel Ramsey was there also?"

"Unluckily for me he was." Chase told Guiterrez everything that had happened. And after this telling, somehow he felt as if a heavy weight had been lifted from his shoulders.

"I know when a man is lying, Señor Donavan. You are not lying. So, the man who accused you of murder is up at Fort Lyon . . . what now?"

"Dammit, I don't know. The army thinks I'm dead, Juan. Maybe I should just leave it that way. Just go on with my life."

"As I'm hoping to go on with mine," murmured Guiterrez. He adjusted the pillow as his wife entered the room to inquire if their guest would be staying for supper.

"No, I'll be heading out."

"I tell you," said Guiterrez, "it isn't easy to let go of

something like this. Could I just walk away?"

"The question is, Juan, has Ramsey struck some deal with the Prairie Cattle Company?"

"If so, many people are in grave danger."

"If he has," Chase said on reflection, "he just might find that I'm not dead after all."

When Chase settled down on the wagon seat and reached for the reins, he heard the clop-clopping of hoofs coming from behind. He turned curiously for a look, and felt a little uneasy when two horsemen swung away from one another as they reined up.

One of them asked, "You be Donavan?"

"Hardcases," he remarked silently. "I could be."

"Smartmouth, I asked if you was Donavan . . . well?"

"You seem to know who I am." Under cover of the wooden back of the seat Chase eased out his sidearm. "Tell me what you want or track out pronto!"

The gunhand allowed a skeptical grin to uncrease his wide mouth. "Bet you feel awful testy now that you gunned down an old pard of mine name of Oberbye. I figure Oberbye got backshot. Nester, I plumb don't like you. As for why we're here—" he nodded up the street—"the bossman wants to see you . . . pronto. . . ."

Casting a wary eye that way, Chase said, "Your bossman is driving an awful fancy rig."

"Mr. MacGregor don't like to be kept waiting, nester."

"MacGregor owns that cattle company. I'll palaver with him." Chase brought his gun up and smiled. "But you two sweethearts ride ahead of me." Scowling, the gunhands spurred down the street, and Chase leathered his gun as he reined away from the edge of the lane.

He studied the man seated in a surrey parked a short distance from a connecting side street. The rig had padded leather seats and open sides, and a fringed frieze ran around the edges of the roof which shaded the man's face. But closing in, Chase could make out watchful pale blue eyes studying him along with the arrogant set to Ian MacGregor's mouth. Everything about the man's expensive clothing spoke of unpretentious wealth, as did the groomed horse hitched to the traces. Chase wheeled alongside the surrey and nodded curtly.

"I say, whatever happened to your face, Mr. Donavan?"

The question gave Chase pause, then resentment tightened his eyes. He said testily, "My pa always said I shouldn't smoke in bed."

"Whatever," the man said casually. "To get to it, as you westerners say, Mr. Donavan, I was told you were in town. So naturally I wanted to see the man who killed those renegades."

"Weren't they working for you, MacGregor?"

"Hardly that."

Deciding to test the waters, Chase said, "Along with others of the same breed. Can't figure someone like you out."

"Really, Mr. Donavan, I'm just a simple businessman. I see out here a chance to make a profit."

"But at what price?"

"At my price," MacGregor said icily. "I have a simple philosophy, Mr. Donavan. Either a man is for me or he's my enemy. The choice is yours."

"A helluva choice is the way I see it. So get to it, MacGregor, I've got a long ride home."

"Home, you say." Ian MacGregor smiled boldly. In

one hand he held the reins, the other rested on a black-enameled cane. "I consider men like you interlopers, Mr. Donavan. Which is my way of saying I'm willing to buy your homestead . . . for a reasonable price."

It came to him then that the Scotsman was hoping he'd explode in anger, which would give MacGregor an opportunity to unleash his hired guns. With the sheriff recovering from his wounds, the only law left in Trinidad, or the county for that matter, was the trio of Mexican deputy sheriffs. This had probably emboldened MacGregor to the point the man felt he had carte blanche when it came to matters of the law. The man had bought off Judge Halloran, according to Juan Guiterrez.

"And if I don't . . . you'll burn me out. . . ."

"Hardly that." MacGregor laughed easily. "Certainly I've heard of how this is happening around the territory. I believe in the sanctity of the law, Mr. Donavan. Just name your price."

McGregor, you're beginning to breathe my air. I can't prove that it's your men who are going after the homesteaders. The same as I don't know if Colonel Ramsey sold out to you. But I'm working on it."

"I consider that a threat."

"Consider it any damned thing you want. Now if you'll excuse me." He lashed his horse into motion, and only felt easier when he'd rounded a corner to place buildings between him and those hired guns of Ian MacGregor.

Back in his surrey, the Scotsman's face revealed to the gunmen his terrible anger, but this was something MacGregor had learned to control. A man like Chase Donavan, he was beginning to realize, could be dangerous if allowed to live. The man was obviously not gun-shy, as were a lot of the homesteaders his men were going against. The man could give strength and more dangerously an organizational bent to his neighbors up along the Purgatoire River. But then there was Donavan's weak point, and Ian MacGregor fastened those cold eyes of his upon the hardcases.

"Matt Traxel will be riding in tonight."

"We can handle that sodbuster just as easy, Mr. MacGregor."

"We'll handle Donavan same as the others."

"A damned shame him just a short distance away and alone. That one's got a smart mouth."

"Gentlemen, if he doesn't want to sell out, consider that he left his wife and son here in Trinidad. A very stupid move on Donavan's part, I'd venture to say."

Chapter Twelve

It galled Sergeant Burl Adamle, his being ordered to go into Las Animas on some fool errand for Lieutenant Stuart. That's what the Indian scouts were for and damnfool privates. The order had just been relayed to him by Sergeant Major Weaver along with the warning not to linger at the High Sky Saloon.

"Shitfire, Sergeant Major, I'm an Indian fighter . . . not some errand boy."

"You sorely trouble me, Adamle, you sorely do. Lately you can't seem to do anything right." The sergeant major thrust his grizzled face close to Burl Adamle's. "All it seems you ever want to do is head out for Trinidad. Damned if I don't think some Mexican woman down there has got her teeth sunk into your mangy hide."

"Lookee here, Hank Weaver, I won't take that sass from no man."

Grizzled laughter bubbled out of the sergeant major's grinning mouth. "I swear, I should have known— damn you, Adamle, you're moonstruck. Just make sure before riding out you don't put your saddle on backward."

"I shall respectfully carry out this damnfool assignment," Adamle muttered. "Here it's colder than your heart, Sergeant Major, and I've got to maybe get frostbit or worse."

"Just bundle up properly so you don't freeze your carrot off. Just to pacify you some, that order came down from the old man himself."

"The colonel?"

"Don't worry, Ramsey didn't pick you out to go in and get that telegram. Another thing that puzzles me, Burl, is that you seem to make yourself scarce whenever the colonel's around. Checked your service record; know you and Ramsey were stationed together down at Fort Randall. Did he court-martial you or something?"

"I was too smart for that."

"Reason you carry them sergeant stripes."

"You can have them if it'll mean me not cutting out for Las Animas."

"Duty calls, Adamle. So hustle into them stables and get saddled and on the way."

It was only five miles to Las Animas, but the beating wind shrilling from behind at Burl Adamle made it seem longer. Lodged in his thoughts as he sat hunkered in the saddle was that a couple of other times when Colonel Ramsey had sent someone into Las Animas to fetch a telegram, shortly thereafter they went out on patrol. The army operated in strange ways sometimes, though not so strangely as to send orders through the Wells-Fargo office.

"Hellfire, standing orders out here are to protect all civilians. Which means patrolling on a regular basis."

His running into Chase Donavan down at Trinidad came into the forefront of his mind. Just seeing Donavan again, especially what had happened to the man's face, had shaken him considerably. He'd been half-expecting Donavan to show up at Fort Lyon and confront Colonel Ramsey. But it was the presence of Ramsey down at Trinidad that occupied Adamle's thoughts now. Every so often homesteaders either fleeing or leaving the territory would stop at Fort Lyon seeking refuge for a day or two. The stories they'd told of what was happening farther south weren't pretty. And up at Fort Lyon at the moment was that delegation of Hispanics and Anglos from the Trinidad area. They wanted protection that Colonel Ramsey seemed reluctant to give.

"Hellfire, the colonel should station a company or two down there."

Instead, whenever they went out on patrol, it was to patches of territorial Colorado that hadn't heard a gun sound in months. The other officers hadn't tried to countermand Colonel Ramsey's strange orders for fear it would hurt their military careers.

"Just a pack of West Pointers. Except for Major K.C. Mitchell."

Mitchell was a former enlisted man who'd earned his commission during the Indian Wars. Adamle knew the man to be a loner, but the men respected him. Trouble was, he pondered, that Mitchell would head out on drinking bouts, along with the cruel fact that Colonel Ramsey considered K.C. Mitchell to be unreliable. Mitchell could be a starting point for his suspicions about the colonel, but to go to the major meant that he needed concrete evidence.

The blustery wind followed Burl Adamle into Las Animas, a much smaller town than Trinidad but also strung along the Purgatoire River. Despite the sergeant major's warning to him, Adamle sought the hitching rail in front of the High Sky Saloon and the warmth inside.

"You lost, Adamle?"

130

"Just give me some whiskey."

"I thought your enlistment was up—"

"Less than a year to go. Damn, that warmed the innards." He crooked a finger and the barkeep refilled his shot glass. "Town seems awful quiet."

"Usually is during the week. I expect you've heard about all that trouble down south. The burnings and all."

"Everyone has." Adamle emptied his glass and left the saloon. He turned his head away from the biting wind as he hurried along the dirt street. A dog bounded off the porch of a mercantile store and came at Adamle with bared fangs. He lashed out with a boot to send it sprawling, and grinned as it slunk away. Just up the street he turned into the telegraph office and waited until another customer had left.

"I'm to pick up a telegram for Colonel Ramsey."

The clerk turned to a desk and shuffled through paperwork until he came up with a brown envelope. "This is for Colonel Ramsey's eyes only," the clerk warned Adamle.

"That so," he came back. "It ain't the colonel has to ride back in this cold weather to Fort Lyon." Adamle folded the letter and slid it into a tunic pocket as he turned toward the door.

He went back toward his horse tied in front of the High Sky Saloon, and instead of climbing into the saddle, Burl Adamle entered the saloon. The same customers were there; a sheepherder sleeping off a drunk at a back table and two locals playing cribbage. Stopping at the bar, he ordered a drink while fingering a pickle out of a large bottle on the bar. With his drink in hand, Adamle found a table close to the pot-bellied stove. He waited until the barkeeper had wandered over to watch those playing cribbage, then Adamle pulled out the envelope and held it over the

131

spout of a coffeepot heating on the stove. It didn't take long for the hot steam issuing from the spout to loosen the sealed flap on the envelope. Finding his seat again, he took out the telegram and unfolded it, and read:

Ramsey

Section cleared between Black Mesa and Raton Pass. Proceed at your discretion.

I.M.

"Now this is a puzzler."

Sergeant Burl Adamle removed the winter campaign hat and ran a troubled hand along his temple. First of all, just what was there down in that area mentioned in this wire? Sorting out the many patrols he'd been on in that general direction, Adamle knew that from Two Buttes and stretching southward there was mostly big ranches while just south of Black Mesa was the Cimarron Cutoff of the Santa Fe Trail. A few rivers creased the prairie down there, and toward the west, toward Raton Pass, lay the cowtown of Raton. Wait a minute, a lot of those homesteaders who'd been passing through had settled in this area.

"Yup," he remarked thoughtfully, "two bits'll get me a double eagle that when Ramsey gets this wire us troopers will be heading down thataway."

Now it began coming together for Burl Adamle, those marauders burning out the homesteaders if they wouldn't sell . . . these wires telling Colonel Ramsey where to send his patrols . . . and Ramsey betraying his trust as an officer. A cold chill seemed to settle between Sergeant Adamle's shoulder blades. The colonel had murdered once down in Texas. Up here in Colorado he'd sold out to someone with the initials

I.M. Which just might be the owner of the Prairie Cattle Company.

"Now what?" pondered the sergeant. "Colonel Ramsey sees I opened this wire he'll come down on me hard. But I need evidence he received it. That photography shop just down the street."

Tramping outside, Adamle hurried past the front of the buildings and the few vacant lots until he found a small board-sided building, the bell above the door chiming as he crossed the threshold and framed a tentative smile for a balding man with round spectacles resting on the bridge of his protruding nose. "You be the photographer?"

"I am Ezra DuCamp."

"I've got a document here that I need photographed . . . just in case I might misplace it. Can you perform that feat?"

"Hmmm, a telegram? And you are?"

"I'm stationed up at Fort Lyon. Ah . . . Sergeant Ramsey."

"I see no problem with making a copy of this. I'll have to charge for it, fifty cents."

Adamle plunked down on a handy chair as the photographer passed through a curtained alcove. As he waited, he deliberated over going back to the Wells-Fargo office. He wanted to find out if that wire had been sent from Trinidad. But that clerk was probably being paid off by Ramsey to keep his mouth shut. So just deliver the telegram to Colonel Ramsey. But once he did, and whereupon orders came for them to patrol that section of land mentioned in the wire, no longer would there be any uncertainties of what to do with his copy of that telegram. He would have to confide in Major K.C. Mitchell. Knowing that his ace in the hole was that he'd seen Colonel Ramsey murder a fellow soldier down in Texas, Burl Adamle felt some of that chill pass away from his shoulder blades. Still, if he was found out, there was every possibility James Ramsey would have one more notch on his service revolver.

"Tomorrow it'll be boots and saddles, men," barked Sergeant Major Hank Weaver upon entering the barracks. "You'll be out on patrol two weeks."

"Whereabouts we going this time?" grumbled a private.

"Heading south and maybe into warm weather."

Burl Adamle stepped over. "Hank, that wouldn't be that Black Mesa country would it?"

"It would, Adamle. You'll find that going down to Las Animas was a picnic compared to this. But an old soldier like you, Adamle, shouldn't have any problems with the cold."

"Hank, you're a real sympathic sonofabitch."

The sergeant major returned Adamle's smile. "Just making sure my troops get their proper exercise."

"Who's in charge this time?"

"Mitchell will be heading this patrol."

"What about Ramsey?"

"Someone has to tend the fires. Reveille'll be at five o'clock. So I suggest you men snuggle in early."

After the sergeant major had left to head over to another barracks, Burl Adamle stepped past his cot and sent troubled eyes looking out a window at the haze of late afternoon. Burning a hole in a tunic pocket was that copy he'd made of the telegram. Something that should have come to mind sooner, at the time he'd been ordered to ride down to Las Animas two days ago, was Colonel Ramsey receiving a telegram at that town. The telegram line extended through Fort Lyon. Perhaps two wires had been sent out, was the only way Adamle could figure it, one coming up here to tell Ramsey of another waiting for him at Las Animas. Whoever was sending these wires and Ramsey were some cautious sonsofbitches, mused Adamle.

What did he know of Colonel James Ramsey? Arrogant, deceitful, besides being disliked by those he commanded. Another thing, the man was a stickler for detail, which to Adamle meant that the colonel could be a sort of pack rat in that he stowed away important papers and documents. These could be found at Ramsey's quarters or at his office adjoining the orderly room. Certainly he would destroy these wires. Unless, and this gave Burl Adamle a ray of hope, he was keeping them just in case his fellow conspirator tried a double cross.

Long after the other cavalrymen had sought a final bout with the bottle over at the army canteen, Sergeant Adamle lay on his cot smoking a tailormade and taking an occasional sip from a bottle of corn liquor he kept hidden in his foot locker. The turnip-shaped watch propped up on his foot locker told him it was going on eleven, and that before midnight the others would come easing back to sack out for the night. He waited another fifteen minutes before turning out the coal oil lamp and leaving the long wooden building.

Burl Adamle strolled along buildings lining the parade grounds. Distantly he could make out the vague outlines of those houses in officer's row. Either Colonel Ramsey would be there or over at the officers' club, but most certainly not at his office, Adamle was hoping. There were no men posted along the walls of the fort, just those on duty at the main gates. Post headquarters was located in a large one-story building, and much to Adamle's relief it was cloaked in darkness. But a short distance away he could hear music coming from the canteen, along with the pale gleam of light seeping out of the windows. The sky was slightly overcast, lighter than usual because of the moon hovering eastward.

"That's a break," Adamle muttered, upon finding the front door unlocked. Quickly he entered to pad silently down a long corridor running the length of the building. Another stroke of luck was the door leading into the orderly room standing open. Easing inside, he closed the door. In the room were four desks, various cabinets, and the closed door beyond which lay Colonel Ramsey's office. But he found the door was locked.

"Man don't even trust his own bladder," he grumbled.

If there was a spare key, it would be in Sergeant Major Weaver's desk, and he stepped there. In a lower drawer his seeking hand touched a ring of keys. A few minutes later he was easing into the colonel's spacious office. Behind the large mahogany desk stood the regimental flag and the Stars and Stripes. A few framed pictures hung on the walls; otherwise they were barren. There was a large bookcase, some cabinets, and a padded sofa. He began his search at the desk. He could have taken his copy of the telegram over to Major Mitchell's quarters, but it was Adamle's notion that he needed more proof than just one wire. If he could find other wires, then determine if they matched where Colonel Ramsey had been sending out patrols, the major would have to believe him.

Adamle froze when footsteps sounded in the corridor. He reasoned that it was probably one of the officers or a sentry going through. And to his disappointment the contents of the desk produced no telegrams. Neither did two of the cabinets. Adamle

136

gazed ruefully at the bookcase, but a couple of strides carried him to the remaining cabinet, one that was smaller and more decorous. And locked, he discovered. The cabinet reposed in a dark corner, and when Adamle went back to the desk, he brought with him a paper clip he'd found in a drawer and a lamp. He'd have to risk lighting the lamp, and when light spread out from the lamp resting on top of the cabinet, he turned his attention to the lock. In his anxiety over having to light the lamp, it seemed forever to Burl Adamle before he had sprung the lock and swung the cabinet doors open. On the top shelf were a holstered gun, a Colt .45, and some boxes of shells, the middle shelf holding a photograph album, but on the bottom shelf lay a leather dispatch pouch used by the army to deliver messages. With a trembling hand he picked it up to pull out its contents. Among the items were yellowed sheafs that could only be telegrams. He separated these from the other papers, to find the top wire was the latest one sent to Colonel Ramsey.

"You pack rat sonofabitch . . . I've got you now."

Sneaking a quick look at the others, he found they contained the same cryptic messages. Hurriedly he left the telegram he'd made a copy of with the other paperwork which he slid back into the pouch. He closed the cabinet doors and doused the light. There was no way he could lock the cabinet, his hope being that Colonel Ramsey might not discover it was unlocked until after they'd left on patrol.

"Anyway, the fat's in the fire now."

Displeasure clouded Major K.C. Mitchell's sleep-filled eyes when he opened the door and found one of his sergeants standing on his front porch. Once upon a not too long ago time the major had been considered on the handsome side of forty. But too many lonely times spent with a bottle had ruddied out his angular face and put purplish veins in his long nose. Yet it was said of K.C. Mitchell that he could still outride and outfight most officers his age, and that included every officer at Fort Lyon. Another reason Adamle had sought out the major was simply that the man had a close rapport with those of lower rank. He'd also borne in mind the deep resentment Colonel Ramsey was always exhibiting for Mitchell.

"Adamle, it's past midnight . . . and we head out into the boonies come sunup. Just what the hell is this all about?" He tucked the other suspender strap over a wide shoulder and motioned for Adamle to enter, then he slammed the door shut and strode to a side table. "Sit, dammit, and get to the gist of it."

"I got me some telegrams here, sir, that have been sent to Colonel Ramsey."

The major reached over for a whiskey bottle. "How the hell did you get your mitts on them?"

"First of all, sir, there's some ancient history got to be cleared up."

"I knew this was going to be a long night. Is this necessary?" He slopped whiskey into a couple of glasses.

"When it involves Colonel Ramsey, it is."

"Seems to me, Sergeant, you two were stationed together down at Fort Randall."

"We was, Major Mitchell, a spell ago. So was an officer name of Lieutenant Chase Donavan."

"Donavan? Hell yes, I ran into Donavan back at . . . Fort Chaffee. Heard he got himself into trouble down in Texas . . . then got himself killed."

"Donavan's one reason I'm here, sir."

"Cut out the sir crap, Adamle, and get to the shank of this."

Adamle cleared his throat, then he grinned wanly and sipped from the glass. "What would you say, Major, if I was to tell you it was Ramsey killed that sergeant down there instead of Donavan."

"I heard it was something like that, Lieutenant Donavan brought up on charges for killing an enlisted man."

"I witnessed the whole thing, sir. We was out on maneuvers . . . up around the Llano Estacado . . . attacked some Comanche. Only there was too many of them. Ramsey chickened out and made a break for it. Sergeant Riddell went after Ramsey just to keep the damned coward from getting killed . . . me coming after. I'd just cleared this ridge and come down upon Ramsey blazing away at Riddell . . . and then Lieutenant Donavan appeared with the other column . . . but it was Donavan alone coming onto Ramsey. Me, I kept back . . . in shock I guess over what had happened. Next thing I *comprendo,* it's Ramsey bringing in a prisoner."

"Donavan?"

"Brought Donavan back to Fort Randall and locked him in the stockade."

"This is a farfetched story, Adamle. To accuse someone, especially one of high rank, of murder. . . ." He gulped down some whiskey as he pondered over this bizarre story of Burl Adamle's. "Too bad Donavan's dead. His testimony and yours could prove interesting."

"That why I'm here, sir. Damned if I don't run into Lieutenant Donavan down at Trinidad."

"That puts a new coat of paint on the barracks," speculated Major Mitchell.

"He's changed, Donavan has, his face being scarred up like that and all and him blinded in one eye. But it's Donavan, alright."

139

"At Trinidad?"

"Got himself a homestead along the Purgatoire, he has, sir."

"So what has this all to do with these telegrams you stole from Colonel Ramsey?"

After asking the major to fetch him a sheet of writing paper and pencil, Burl Adamle drew a rough map of the territory under the protective jurisdiction of Fort Lyon. As best he could, Adamle went on to explain how these telegrams tied in with places they had patrolled in the past few weeks.

"See here, Major, we were sent out west, around the Rattlesnake Buttes, when all this trouble was breaking out down south. Then up past the Arkansas to Ordway and beyond. Now this latest wire mentions Raton Pass and Black Mesa. Is it just coincidence us heading out thataway tomorrow?"

"This is interesting."

"Why down there, sir? Maybe it's because those who've been marauding the country have cleared out most of the homesteaders down there. Here they've been murdering folks while Colonel Ramsey has issued orders detailing us elsewhere. Dammit, Major, it's the same as if Ramsey himself has been killing these people."

"This is damning talk, Adamle," Mitchell said quietly. "But these wires are also damning. Divisional headquarters up at Denver would have to be told about this. The only thing is, it'll be your word against Ramsey's . . . as to the explanation behind these telegrams . . . and just who did murder that sergeant down in Texas. This means we need to palaver with Chase Donavan."

"This eases my mind a lot, sir."

"Come morning, Adamle, we'll head out on patrol. Proceed as ordered down to Black Mesa. On the way back we'll detour over to see Donavan. As for these wires, I'll stow them in my saddlebags. You know . . . I've been sizing you up as we've been talking. Carrying around the truth of what Ramsey did down there can get awful heavy after a while. Ramsey, a real mean bastard. A traitor to those who've been killed lately."

"It'll ease my mind a lot, Ramsey getting his just reward."

"Now hit the sack, Sergeant, and speak to no one about this. The other officers consider me nothing more than a maverick. I've learned to accept this . . . as you've learned to live with what you know about our esteemed colonel. So sleep tight, Adamle."

Chapter Thirteen

Chase Donavan had been in a dark mood when he'd gotten back from Trinidad. And with Raven and the boy there, it wasn't too long before the homestead became a lonely place. Oftentimes as Chase was putting up a pole corral he would make up his mind to go after Colonel James Ramsey, then simmer down and take out his bitterness by toiling away with the post-hole digger. You just couldn't ride up to Fort Lyon and gun down an officer and expect to get away. Before, getting away wouldn't have entered into it.

No sooner had autumn passed away than they were enjoying a lengthy spell of Indian Summer, which had come after a light snowfall and frost had set into the ground. Vari-colored leaves lay thick under the barren trees; when trod upon they were set to rustling. The sun stood more to the south, and cast a subdued mellowy glow. Chase also took in the mare's tail sky, the threads of wispy cirrus clouds telling him they were in for a long spate of fine weather.

Sweat stained his woolen shirt and came salty to sting at his left eye, though sometimes there came a phantom pain from the empty socket which once encased his right. No hair would grow on the burned portion of his face, so he'd gotten to calling himself with some amusement the half-shaved man. Slowly he was coming to grips with his disfigurement. Then he'd been spotted by Sergeant Burl Adamle down at Trinidad.

Could it be pride now, he wondered, that made him want to go after Ramsey. He set the post-hole digger aside and wrestled a log over and dropped one end into the deep hole. As Chase shoveled dirt back into the hole to help support the log, he knew chiefly that most of it had to do with clearing his name. Forever in the annals of military history he would be listed as a murderer and deserter. A heavy price to pay for someone else. With the hole filled with loose dirt and spilling over some, he used his boot to tamp it hard around the log while making certain it was lined up straight with the others. Then he decided, no sense brooding over what he was gonna do or not do about Colonel Ramsey.

Just yesterday a patch of folks from around Trinidad had crossed over from the river road and asked Chase if they could camp over for the night. Seems they'd been up to Fort Lyon, delegated to go there by their neighbors in an attempt to have the army send down some troops. Their bitter conversation had gone like this.

"It is against army policy . . . Colonel Ramsey told us."

"*Si*," explained another Hispanic. "No *soldados* can be spared to protect us from these banditos."

"But we all know who is behind this."

"The big cattlemen."

"What about Sheriff Guiterrez?"

"Guiterrez is still laid up. But there are rumors about some of his deputies . . . that they work for this cattle company."

"What about you, Juan Vasquez, if these men come

143

and ask you to sell your place . . . ?"

"What choice do I have other than to give these men what they want. There is my wife . . . my five *niños*."

Chase could still see the fear in Juan Vasquez's eyes as he headed toward the house. Before their departure this morning a message had been relayed to Chase that Hilario Madrid wanted to see him. It was probably Hilario wanting to sell him some cattle. Finishing the corral could wait as Chase wanted a taste of good Mex cooking. He considered Madrid and the others up there more than just friends. These people had hacked a good living out of barren nothingness, this in country more accustomed to seeing wild cattle rambling around or game animals. As the country settled more, Chase envisioned the children of these people marrying Anglos, or even Jesse Keepseagle courting an Hispanic woman. He considered his neighbors equals. Maybe he was alone in this thinking as a lot of Anglos considered an Hispanic to be no better than a Comanche or Ute.

But Chase's true purpose for heading up to Madrid's plaza was to make these people aware of the coming dangers, and of their need to band together when that time came. More than one homesteader passing through had ridden in to seek some drinking water and detail to Chase what was happening, while Ian MacGregor's looking him up at Trinidad told Chase he was a marked man.

"Could be I'm the lightning rod that's gonna draw a lot of trouble in the days to come."

"You are some craftsman, Jacob."

"It seems, my good friend, I can express myself better with my hands."

144

On the way up the river road Chase had detoured over to Jacob Purcell's small homestead. In the large shed just newly completed by Jacob the pelts of small game animals were heaped in neat piles. But it was the workmanship detailed in the framework around the door and windows that held Chase's attention. This building was made to last, and Chase knew that in time Jacob and his son would raise bountiful crops.

"Its a shame you didn't bring your family."

"Part of why I came here, Jacob. They're living in Trinidad, mostly because Jesse needs some schooling."

"Yes, one can't get far in life without an education. Clara has taken over that chore. Something our children don't take kindly to. And I believe you stopped by, Chase, to warn me about what's been happening."

"I know some of these homesteaders leaving the territory have stopped here too, Jacob. What troubles me is that the army seems reluctant to give us any protection. And when it comes, it's too late."

"We have some weapons, Chase. At any rate, we'll give a good account of ourselves if those marauders show up. You said you were on your way up to see Hilario Madrid . . . ?"

"To get his opinion on what to do. We need to band together until this trouble is over."

"Sorry, Chase, but I won't ride with you. Simply because my place is here. Clara feels the same way." Jacob Purcell stepped outside and inhaled deeply of the still air as his eyes savored the high sky beyond the river. "There's something about this place gets to a man."

"Maybe it's just having the Rockies for neighbors. But I know what you mean, Jacob." To the west a barren meadow passed onto the main road while stands of oak and elm trees and a few cottonwoods guarded the homesteader's buildings. Unlike Chase's homestead, everyone passing by had a clear view of this place. In a way its location was like Jacob, open, trusting, a place at peace with all it surveyed. The only trouble was a lot of passersby viewed it with greedy minds. Jacob Purcell was leaving himself open to terrible retribution by not taking his family to Trinidad until matters had run their bloody course out here. It had settled in Chase's bones that trouble was just over the horizon for him, Jacob, and Madrid and his people. He would discuss with Hilario, even if Chase had to pay for it, the possibility of sending a few men down here. At this point in time foolish heroics could get the Purcells killed, since he realized that Jacob would die rather than move on.

It seemed strange to see peaceful men going around carrying long guns. Another safeguard taken by Hilario Madrid was his plaza keeping their horses corraled instead of turning them loose to graze in Red Rock Canyon. Chase had been challenged when fording the Purgatoire to respond in Spanish before being allowed to cross over and make for the settlement. He ran a gauntlet of yapping dogs as he drew up near Hilario idling by a corral with two other men.

"You expecting trouble?"

Hilario laughed, and said calmly, "Always. Did you come here about the cattle?"

He'd learned from Hilario that cattle could be winter grazed in the many canyons strung along the river. This was ideal country for that purpose and why, he assumed, others were casting covetous eyes this way. He felt some of his loneliness peel away when Hilario's wife sang out that supper was ready.

"I expect you to spend the night, El Condor."

"Expect I'll do that," responded Chase as he turned

his horse loose in the corral. Dropping his saddle by a corral post, he fell into step with the others.

Although he'd gotten used to Raven's cooking, what he had for supper—refried beans and tacos—made Chase heap his plate a second time. The conversation going on around him was a mixture of broken English and Spanish as these men discussed the cruel injustices being imposed upon the homesteaders.

"The *soldados* . . . they are useless as tits on a bull. . . ."

"All because of who's commanding up at Fort Lyon."

"They have never protected us anyway."

"*Si*, Gomez, neither will the ranchers we work for care too much if we get wiped out. So what shall it be, my friend? Do we stand up for our rights or . . . crawl away like coyotes?"

"Hilario," Chase said, "I know you won't run. Neither will anyone else. The ones we've got to worry about are those hired by the Prairie Cattle Company . . . men posing as deputy sheriffs."

"I have gotten wind of this. Go on."

"They'll ask you to sell out. Those who don't . . . get gunned down and burned out. The leader of this pack of cutthroats is a man named Matt Traxel—a genuine gunfighter. Takes his orders from Ian MacGregor, bossman of this cattle company."

Hilario Madrid's wife brought over a bottle of tequila as he said, "*Quizas* we should hold these starpackers hostage if they show up. Maybe geld them before sending them back to Trinidad."

The eyes of everyone at the large round table threw out sparks of silent laughter. But beneath this, Chase could detect, lurked a resentment deeper than the one he had for Colonel James Ramsey. Behind them in the fieldstone fireplace burned a few short logs sending out heat and exploding sparks of light. Many a time Chase had sat before that fireplace, just him and Hilario Madrid. Many a time Hilario had cast him comforting words as they shared a bottle of tequila. Sometimes it would be Hilario or him going under from too much tequila, with morning sunlight jarring their heavy lids open. He had found Hilario Madrid to be a wise man. Some of those words had wormed their way into Chase's mind to help change his way of looking at this cruel world. Now it was coming full circle again, his past coming back in the form of James Ramsey, but this time Chase was determined to bury it for good.

"I tried to talk Jacob Purcell into taking his family to Trinidad until this is over. Wouldn't hear of it."

"Señor Purcell is a *testarudo* man."

"Too damned stubborn," agreed Chase. "Maybe, Hilario, some of your people could stay at my place for a while. I'd be most pleased to hire them on."

"That could be arranged. It is true they could use the money . . . but that would be between you and them. Perhaps they could help you with those cattle you came to buy." Madrid had a crafty smile for his guest.

"No wonder you're patron here. Didn't plan on herding them down yet, Hilario."

"I have fifty head waiting to go."

"Don't need any bulls."

"These are mostly cows . . . and a few steers."

"Might's well take them." He let one of the Mexicans refill his glass. "Say for twenty dollars a head."

"In greenbacks, I trust."

"Gave up on trying to pass Confederate money."

When they trailed out a little past sunup it was Chase and three of Madrid's *compadres*. Along about midmorning the stagecoach from Trinidad rambled

148

past on its northward passage to Old Las Animas and points farther on. Other than this, traffic on the vague ribbon of road was almost nonexistent but for some cowhands loping their horses the way the cattle were walking. The vaqueros hired by Chase were of varying ages: Chico in his twenties, if that; the older one a stoop-shouldered Mex who from observation by Chase knew his way around cattle; lastly there was Jose, having a flowing mustache and probably in his middle thirties. He let the older one, Rafael, handle the point, and saw no need of anyone riding drag as the cattle tended to let the wind carry them along rather than get it into their heads to hang back.

Reining up by Jose, Chase said, "Off to the east I spotted chimney smoke."

"Last year, Señor Donavan, you would have seen no smoke."

"Meaning it's a homestead."

Nodding, Jose said, "Most of the year that creek sees so little water even the coyotes do not go there to drink. These people will no doubt leave before too much longer."

"What do you think of all this?"

"I do not like to be forced from my land. It is as simple as that, Señor Donavan."

"Nobody does. Which is why all this killing is going on. Another mile or two and we'll pass Jacob's place. His place is too much out in the open, Jose. I'm glad you and the others threw in with me."

"Don't worry, Senor Donavan, we'll take turns watching that homestead."

"I wish there was more I could do."

"You are doing all you can . . . as we are. The big ranchers have many, many guns. Only the army can handle all that has happened."

"Around here the army is getting a bad name, Jose.

And I don't like it any more than you do or Hilario does. I'm hoping that when winter really sets in these marauders will hang close to town or vamoose . . . because not too many hardcases cotton to snow and the like. By the way, do you or any of the others cook?"

"Rafael has handled that *empleo* from time to time. But what of your cooking, señor?"

"You cotton to sowbelly —"

"*Que va,* I hope Rafael does not turn us down."

Chapter Fourteen

The soldiers from Fort Lyon felt a helluva lot better when the order came to head out. Bivouacking at this homestead had been the major's idea. All through the moonlit night they'd been too aware of the charred remains of the buildings and three crosses marking grave sites. South of Two Buttes was where the destruction started. Then down at Springfield, purely a cowtown, they'd received a cold reception. Knowing he couldn't get a nickel's worth of information from these people, Major K.C. Mitchell had simply left town.

The only living creatures spotted by the patrol thereafter had been a lot of grazing cattle and the usual run of antelope. During the morning the major didn't say much until they were easing around Mesa de Maya and he had set his sights on the elevations around Raton Pass.

"Adamle, so far we haven't encountered one homesteader. Those bastards didn't burn the places of those who sold out."

"These cattlemen probably intend to use them as line camps, sir."

"Awful convenient for these murderers. A lot of this could have been avoided if Colonel Ramsey hadn't

151

sold out."

"Hope those telegrams are enough evidence."

"If they aren't, Adamle, there's Chase Donavan."

After flowing down into a gully and riding back onto prairie, Major Mitchell and Adamle looked at one another upon sighting horses idling in a corral near a small bunch of buildings. "What do you make of it?"

"Sure wouldn't be any homesteader."

"Yeah, no question about that." Mitchell swung up an arm. "Johnson, take ten men and come in from the north. The rest stay with me." He spurred on as his troopers fanned their horses out in a skirmish line. The hard alkali ground spurted up gusts of dust. At Mitchell's command to unlimber their rifles, the troopers pulled them out of saddle boots. Then the major eased his walking horse past the corral.

"It's about noon, sir," Adamle commented.

"Probably chowing down in that sodhouse spewing out chimney smoke."

"There's a half dozen horses in that corral."

"Could be just some cowhands using this as a line camp. But we'll sure as hell find out. Corporal Turner . . . sound reveille."

"Reveille, sir?"

"My intentions, corporal, are to wake these bastards up."

Grinning now, the corporal brought the brass bugle to his lips and sounded the call. This caused the horses in the corral to prance away in alarm and a lonely cowpuncher to burst out of the sodhouse. His confused eyes took in the ring of cavalrymen.

"What the hell . . . is this?"

Two more cowhands emerged from the house, one grasping his Winchester, and sighting this, Major Mitchell barked, "Drop that rifle or I'll order my men to fire!"

The rifle clattered down at the cowhand's feet. "I . . . I thought the army was here to fight Indians . . . not some lowly cowpokes. . . ."

"If that's what you are, gents."

"We is, Major. We was told to drift some cattle out thisaway . . . and headquarters here."

"What outfit do you work for?"

"That cattle company out of Trinidad."

"What do you think, Adamle?"

"One of them isn't even wet behind the ears. Just three cowpokes hired on at forty a month and found. But we sure scared the hell out of them."

The skeptical glimmer left the major's eyes as he said, "Would that be the Prairie Cattle Company?"

"Yup, sir, that she be."

"What happened to the people who built this place?"

"Gone is all we know."

In an aside to Adamle the major said, "We'll learn nothing here." He spurred on to leave the task of getting the patrol on the move to Sergeant Adamle.

"Our orders were to stay away from Raton or Trinidad," Adamle reminded the major.

"Countermanding the colonel's orders is the only way we'll be able to get a handle on things, Sergeant."

"Place hasn't much size to it." Burl Adamle and the other troopers relaxed in their saddles as Major Mitchell swung down. His eyes slid past a billboard adorning the front wall of a mercantile store and to the man just stepping out of the jail. "Are you the marshal here?"

"That . . . and tax collector of Raton too, mister. Just what the hell is the U.S. Army doing down here?"

"You are?"

"Marshal Stockwell," the man snorted. "Reckon I know why you're here, Major. It's about these burnings."

"What can you tell me about them?"

"Major, this is a cowtown, pure and simple. Maybe I resent all these nesters choking the land as they've been doing, but nobody here would stoop so low as to make war on women and children."

"That include the ranchers?"

"Can't speak for them, Major. But I've heard rumors. And it just could be that repeating these rumors could get me killed. Meaning this job don't pay enough for me to stick my neck out. But you can ask around town, Major. Your privilege . . . seeing as how the army controls this territory anyway."

Pivoting around, Mitchell strode back to his horse and gazed up at Burl Adamle. On his bronzed face lingered a tight smile. "Figured I wouldn't get anything out of the marshal . . . or probably anybody else for that matter. These people are running scared. But the fact that we were here will get around. It won't be long before our esteemed colonel receives another telegram."

"He won't like getting this one. Sir, I've spotted at least two cafes . . . and a change of diet would sure be welcomed."

"How far to Trinidad?"

"As the crow flys . . around fifteen miles."

"That should get us in there just before supper. Just past noon; tell the men to grab some hardtack and jerky out of their saddlebags as we'll be chowing down in the saddle."

"Believe they heard you, sir."

The major brought his patrol away from the buildings and along the winding road leading to Raton Pass. Once the town had fallen behind, he glanced at Adamle and said, "I suspect those telegrams received by Colonel Ramsey were sent from Trinidad. More so, Adamle, since he ordered us to stay away from there. And what Trinidad has are a lot of Hispanics— people who won't be afraid to tell us what's going on—and, Sergeant, a certain Spanish woman."

Burl Adamle felt the blood rushing to his face.

The major went on. "I believe her name is Marie."

"How'd . . . how'd you know that, sir?"

"The sergeant major discussed it with me is how. You plan on getting hitched, Adamle?"

"Figured doing so after my enlistment is up."

"Had a young filly in my sights once. Was a sergeant at the time. Then the army had to dangle a commission before me. Think about her a lot; one of the reasons I have my bouts with the bottle. So if you hanker a lot for this Marie, make sure you don't lose her, Sergeant."

A lot of hostile eyes watched the cavalrymen from Fort Lyon passing along the streets of Trinidad. Where most of the Hispanics lived, along the outskirts of town, a woman's questioning eyes soon picked out Sergeant Burl Adamle.

"He is here," Marie Cordova said to her mother.

"But not to see you it seems. Are you sure this Anglo wants to marry you, Marie?"

"Burl has spoken of that."

"And now that you are with child?"

To conceal her sudden fear Maria Cordova brought the shawl up and covered her head. Her mother was only reminding Maria that too often an Anglo just wanted to bed a Mexican woman. As a result some of

155

the foolish young women had given birth to half-bloods, the woman to be shunned by her people, the child wanted by neither race. This would not happen to her, for all Burl Adamle could talk about was getting married. But she could feel her heart beating faster under the thin protection of her white blouse. If he came to her *casa,* and he must come, how would Burl react to the news he was going to be a father. Marie knew that he must be told, that there must be no secrets between them, otherwise no bond of trust would ever seal their love.

Thirty men not including Sergeant Adamle and the major comprised the patrol, and upon nearing the small downtown area of Trinidad, some of the soldiers dropped off at a livery stable as the others headed toward another stable to leave their horses. Afterwards, orders from Major Mitchell brought them strolling onto main street and toward the Colorado Hotel.

"This is gonna be a treat staying at the Colorado." Adamle beamed.

"Our presence there, Sergeant, is gonna attract a lot of attention. I'm figuring some won't like it. That was a good idea of yours sending some men over to keep an eye on the telegraph office."

"I'll have them relieved after we've chowed down, sir."

"Sergeant, after we've chowed down you have my permission to . . . call upon that woman you've been courting."

"Why, Major, thank you."

"Or you could head over there right now. I'll make sure they save you a bed over at the hotel."

"Obliged, sir." With an eager smile for the major, Burl Adamle swung off the boardwalk and hurried down the street.

"Since when has the army, Major, taken to putting soldiers up at hotels?"

About a half hour ago Major Mitchell had found a table in the dining room at the Colorado Hotel, one quietly placed in a corner and allowing him a glimpse of main street. He had ordered the house special, roast beef, along with requesting the waitress bring him a drink from the barroom. When the shadow had fallen upon his table, Mitchell had looked up to see a lanky cattleman standing there.

"From your tone of voice, sir, you don't like it," he said flatly.

"No need to get testy about it, Major. But for some time the army has been shying away from these parts. I'm Easley; got a small spread just to the northwest. Reason I asked, I spent some time serving under General Miles—just another saddle humper."

With the toe of his boot Mitchell shoved a chair away from the table. "Ease down if you've got a minute."

Jackknifing onto the chair, the cattleman tipped his hat back and regarded Major Mitchell through pondering eyes. "Upstairs," he drawled, "resides the man responsible for a lot of our troubles. Country hasn't been the same since Ian MacGregor showed up."

"That's interesting," said Mitchell. "He own that cattle company?"

"About it. Has hired himself some hardcases, Major. Got the county judge in the palm of his hand."

"What about your sheriff; Guiterrez, I believe?"

"Just getting his legs back after being shot. But one man can't stop what's been happening. Couldn't afford it but I hired on some men. And I'll kill anybody that chances onto my land."

"You'll have to understand, Easley, this is my first trip down here. Before it's always been Colonel Ramsey handling any disurbances in these parts. But I gather it's MacGregor behind all of this."

"MacGregor and the cattle barons, damn them." Easley uncoiled from the chair to tower over the table. "Proving that is another matter."

"Appreciate you stopping by, Easley. Once I get a more detailed idea of what's happening, things'll change."

"I hope hell doesn't freeze over first."

Ian MacGregor could scarcely believe his eyes when that army patrol rode brazenly into Trinidad. News of it had been brought to him by Matt Traxel. The gunfighter had just left his rooming house with a few things packed in his saddlebags. But he had taken his own good time about saddling his horse and bringing the bad news to MacGregor. His dislike for the Scotsman had become almost intolerable, feelings that he'd veiled behind his passive countenance. Later on, when this was over, he just might find out what the Scotsman was made of.

"Is Ramsey pulling some kind of doublecross?" raged MacGregor "Here we're all set to go against those intruders living north along the Purgatoire, now this has to happen."

"I wouldn't let it bother me none," Traxel drawled.

"That's it, Traxel, nothing seems to bother you. Only that you get paid on time. Here I've hired on more men . . . at considerable expense, I might add."

"Murder doesn't come cheap, MacGregor."

"The men, where are they camped?"

"Up where the Purgatoire crooks to the east; and getting damned tired of it. Why all this pussyfooting around when we could be up burning and killing along with getting a poke or two."

"How you lived this long, Traxel, I'll never fully understand. But you're right . . . that area must be cleaned out . . . still the army being here. . . ."

"Could be they've just circled around after patrolling down south and stopped here for the night. Know I would instead of sleeping on the hard ground if a nice feather bed was available."

"Whatever, Traxel. Are you ready to leave?"

"Just say the word."

"Have those three deputies go on ahead." Clasping his hands behind him, MacGregor paced over and stared down at the street. "The first place they'll stop is at Chase Donavan's. I believe that once he's out of the way things'll go easier."

"Hell, I could just gun him down and save all this pissing around."

"Perhaps . . . but I'll need to use his buildings as a line camp. No, have the deputies call on Donavan first."

Out behind the Colorado Hotel, Matt Traxel climbed aboard his bronc and reined away. He didn't mind leaving Trinidad, as he'd been dropping a lot of chips at poker, probably lost over a thousand dollars in the last few days. He went down another alleyway, rode past an outhouse guarding the upper reaches of town, and found a trail marked by some cottonwoods. I would take him about an hour to reach the others camped along the river. He didn't mind night riding as much as some. He felt it gave him time to sort out his thoughts as he was doing now, about just how he could outsmart Ian MacGregor. Matt Traxel wanted a bigger share of the pot.

"Man's laid claim to over a million acres. So he'd better divvy up with some more money, or for me it'll mean a trip to Denver to call upon the U.S. Marshal there." Engrossed in his thoughts, the gun-fighter didn't realize he'd been followed ever since leaving the Colorado Hotel.

Back about a quarter of a mile, Deputy Sheriff Tafoya watched the hardcase loping his horse toward the river shining under moonlight. Tafoya had scouted out the outlaw camp Traxel was heading for, and it angered him that he'd spotted those deputies.

"They wear the badge only to fool the people," Tafoya retorted as he brought his bay around and sent it cantering back toward town.

Lately Sheriff Guiterrez had begun taking charge of things, though he still let his deputies handle most of his duties. And the passage of a half hour found Tafoya dismounting before the sheriff's spacious house. As he went up the walkway, Guiterrez rose from where he'd been taking his ease on the front porch.

"Traxel has left to join the others."

"So MacGregor wants the killing to start again. With the soldiers here, Tafoya, I see no need to get a posse together. Who's commanding them?"

"A major, Juan. You'll find him at the hotel."

"*Extrano* that Colonel Ramsey isn't here. But no matter."

"I am still angry at what this colonel is doing, Juan."

"Because of him many people have been killed. When the time comes, justice will prevail. Now I must go to the hotel."

After strolling around town Major K.C. Mitchell had gone up to his room and pulled a bottle of corn liquor out of his saddlebag before duffing his outer garments. Easing onto the narrow bed, he pulled off

160

his black cavalry boots, the spurs chinking softly as he tossed them aside. The talk with that cattleman had whet his desire to look up the sheriff in the morning and get some cold facts. So far the marauders hadn't left anyone alive to testify against them. But if they were headquartered here at Trinidad, at least this would be a starting point.

"Lousy weather anyway," he groused, pulling his suspenders away from his shoulders so that they dangled by his faded blue trousers. There came a soft rapping at the door as he opened the whiskey bottle. Grimacing, he stepped there and swung the door open.

"Major, I'm sorry to disturb you at such a late hour."

"By your badge you must be the sheriff."

"Juan Guiterrez. May I come in?" At a nod from Mitchell he entered and eased the door shut. "It has been some time since the army has sent any *soldados* down here."

Mitchell sat down in one of the chairs at the table and sipped from the bottle. Waiting until Guiterrez was seated, he said, "To tell you the truth, Sheriff, my orders were to avoid coming into Trinidad."

"Orders given by Colonel Ramsey?"

Speculation danced in Mitchell's probing eyes.

Sheriff Guiterrez went on, "I found this out through someone who's settled in here a short while ago."

"Chase Donavan, I figure." He slid the bottle over to Guiterrez.

"*Si*, it was Donavan." Guiterrez hesitated, then around a smile he drank from the bottle. "You must know something about him too, Major?"

"Just that he's considered dead and buried by the army. Accused of a crime committed by my esteemed colonel."

"He told me all of this. I believe Donavan's side of the story. But to get at your colonel . . . and the man behind most of our troubles . . . one must have proof."

"I'm working on that."

"But for now, Major Mitchell, we must forget your colonel. My deputies have been keeping watch on those hardcases working for MacGregor's cattle company. Earlier this week they left town—now their leader has gone to join them."

"Are these the ones responsible for raiding homesteads?"

"So far no one has come forth to *acusar* them. My men have kept watch on their camp farther east along the Purgatoire."

"Should be no trouble finding them."

"Some of them have been over at the cantinas . . . gambling and doing their whoring. They talk carelessly, as though these men feel the law cannot touch them."

"Obliged to you, Guiterrez, for confiding in me."

"I judge a man by what I see in his eyes, Major Mitchell."

"Considering mine have been stained by the sins of whiskey and long bouts with cards, Sheriff, I thank you." Mitchell fished a box of snuff out of his shirt pocket. Prying the lid away, he fingered out some and tucked it inside his right cheek. When Guiterrez had arrived, the whiskey bottle had been almost full, and to his surprise the major now tallied they'd only emptied it down to the halfway mark. Maybe it was the chance of getting back at Colonel James Ramsey that had dulled the edge of his drinking. Slipping into his thoughts was the story narrated to him by Sergeant Adamle. The words of Sheriff Guiterrez confirmed not only what the colonel had done back in Texas but added weight to the man's becoming involved with the

Prairie Cattle Company. "A damned Judas."

"*Perdone?*"

"Just setting my mind frame upon Colonel Ramsey. I can live with Ramsey quilling nasty reports in my service record, Sheriff . . . but knowing he's sullied how you folks hereabouts feel about us cavalrymen . . . that I won't stand for. Getting back to when the colonel was down here, Sheriff Guiterrez, there was this big shindig."

"Those with the power were here, the XIT, Spade, Lone X, Matador. But that these cattle barons would listen to Ian MacGregor." Guiterrez's thick black brows furrowed over his eyes. "Perhaps it was because they felt threatened by . . . change, their vision of the future."

"Barbed wire choking off the open ranges. And the innards of civilization, the Homestead Act, a maverick brand to men used to calling the turn of the card." Mitchell trickled tobacco juice onto the hardwood floor. "They're guilty as sin too. But not as bloodthirsty as this bastard of a Scotsman. Guiterrez, we'll pull out before sunrise."

"Then may God be watching over you."

Chapter Fifteen

Sometimes at night Cristobal Baca could see the distant reflection of lights coming from Trinidad. The plaza he'd started many years ago was located farther north along the Purgatoire, and had grown from five to eleven houses. Lately he had trouble sleeping because of what encroaching age was doing to his wiry frame. Perhaps, Baca had often mused, he should go see the doctor in Trinidad. But that would take money he didn't have. So Cristobal Baca let the aching vagaries of his illnesses slowly ravage his body. A deeply religious man, Baca knew the Lord only allotted everyone so many years.

"Still, to take a leak without feeling pain would be a blessing."

This was what·had brought Cristobal Baca out of his bed. But even as he slipped the heavy shirt over his thinning shoulders, the gray-haired Mexican wondered why some of the dogs were yapping. It could be a coyote or mountain lion was nearby. On sandaled feet he padded out the back door and, as always at this time, lifted his eyes to the sky, a benedictive glance.

"So, *Dios,* I have survived another night."

The darker glow of night was penetrated by a

lighter paleness. Hugging the ground were patches of mist, spilling around the trees and in lower pockets of land. A dog appeared and growled at Baca relieving himself, caught the man's scent and swung away. Then the hound dog belonging to Jesus Valdez began sounding.

"Could it be?" With a deep concern Cristobal Baca's eyes gaped open. All of them here at the plaza were aware of the dangers being brought upon others by these marauders. Over to Baca's left a splash of light came from one of the houses.

"Baca, is that you?"

The words Cristobal Baca were about to fling back caught in his throat as something slammed into his midriff. Staggering backward, he suddenly realized blood was spurting over his white shirt. He sagged onto his knees, knew that his worst fear was coming true, and fell dying to the ground.

The men led by Matt Traxel rushed on foot out of the shadows and broke into the houses. The last hour of night heard the muffled reports of guns, and the screams of both women and children. A few got away by bolting out of houses and into underbrush or the lifting mist. The particular targets of the killers were the men of the plaza. And when this was accomplished there were the women, some already dead, the few who'd been caught now finding themselves at the mercy of lusting men.

After a while Matt Traxel's hardcases began setting fire to the buildings. When they left it was to retrieve their horses and lope easterly along the river. With them had been the three deputy sheriffs, themselves willing participants in the rape and burning of the plaza.

"Are you sure," one of them said, "MacGregor

165

wanted it this way?"

"His own words," said Matt Traxel. He considered it of little importance telling his men that soldiers from Fort Lyon were down at Trinidad. Back of Traxel as he rode were pillars of smoke rising from the burning buildings. The fire would be a warning to others that they were trespassers. Some would leave, and others would make a stand against him, something he welcomed. "Anyway, my way is quicker."

To Major K.C. Mitchell and his men it seemed as if all hell had broken loose farther east along the river. About two hours before sunup they'd left Trinidad, guided by deputy sheriff Tafoya. Tafoya had brought them away from the river and past the floodplain to the beginnings of a ravine, only to find the men they sought were gone. In an abandoned shack snugged against a rocky bluff, embers still flared in the fireplace, and whiskey bottles and other debris littered the floor. Shortly thereafter flames began staining the dark sky, and hurriedly they swung to the east at a gallop.

After a while the reddish glow caused Major Mitchell to bring his men away from the river and go cantering over an elevation. There was no need to hurry now, with the plaza spread out before them. Tafoya began cursing in Spanish when he rode past a woman cradling her dead son, and by unspoken accord everyone swung down and stared in helpless anger at the burning buildings.

"We'll need to find out who did this," said the major.

"*Si*," barked Tafoya, "we must hunt these dogs down and hang them. I come here at times. But this is . . . beyond *comprendering*."

166

"There's a lot of bodies lying around," said the major. "We just can't ride off and leave those who've survived. Break out what bandages and medicine you've got, men."

"Sir," Burl Adamle muttered, "I figured whoever did this will leave a wide trail to follow."

"The only trouble is, Adamle, we're expected back at Fort Lyon. Shouldn't be over this way at all. But we're here . . . so let's pitch in and see what we can do. And detail some of the men to begins digging graves. You, Anderson, ride back to Trinidad and fetch the doctor. There'll probably be others who'll volunteer to come out here. But it's the doctor we need now."

During the long morning as the soldiers tended to both the wounded and the dead it warmed into the low fifties. As Burl Adamle knelt by an older man who'd been shot in the chest, he felt a tightness in his throat when a soldier carried a wounded girl past him. Over by a shed which had somehow survived the burning one of the women who'd been raped simply sat there, her eyes still glazed by her ordeal. Once in a while she would moan while rocking back and forth and folding her arms over her heaving bosom. Being raped had been part of it; learning that her husband and baby had been killed by those terrible predators had sent her into shock. The same thing could have happened to Marie, Adamle knew, a thought which sickened him.

"Damn you, Colonel Ramsey!"

The man he was tending touched his arm, and when Burl Adamle glanced down, it was to see the old man's head sag to one side as he expelled a final gust of air. At that moment Adamle wanted to cry, to shout out his rage at these ruthless killers, but through grief-stricken eyes he simply reached out a hand and closed the dead man's eyes.

"Go with *Dios, amigo.*"

The afternoon seemed to pass even slower. Just before noon the doctor had arrived in his buggy trailed by some townspeople. But more arrived as the sun began its westward trekking of the hazy blue sky. Through the voice of deputy sheriff Tafoya, Major Mitchell was able to acquire descriptions of some of the killers. Mitchell didn't tell Tafoya or the men who'd survived that he would have to report back the details of this massacre to his commanding officer. But he damnwell meant to come back and track down those who did this.

"You've been a great help, Deputy Tafoya."

"If only we could have gotten here in time. But that is the luck of it. We'll use what wagons we found to get those who survived down to Trinidad. This is a bitter day, Major."

"I just hope they don't get a notion to up and lynch Ian MacGregor."

"For certain, Major, he is behind this. But Judge Halloran and the county commissioners don't see it that way. Perhaps it is because they are Anglos and I'm Mexican that I talk this way."

"No, Tafoya, we both know the truth of it. I promise we'll be back."

"Your colonel, Ramsey, I was told about him by Sheriff Guiterrez . . . that the colonel has sided with MacGregor."

"Seems he has. But I aim to brace Ramsey when I get back to Fort Lyon. What about Matt Traxel and his men?"

"What happened here will scare out a lot of homesteaders. Perhaps they'll hole up for a while. . . ."

"Let's hope so."

"Traxel knew that you were in Trinidad, Major, so he'll try and hide his trail. You asked about Chase Donavan. Donavan's place is a few miles past where the river bends to the north. Donavan was here years ago."

"Didn't know that."

"My people began calling him El Condor. This was because the gods who guard the hogback let him live. Great lightning storms hit there, so even wild animals shun the place when it's storming."

"Did he mention being a soldier?"

"Only Hilario Madrid knows the story of Donavan. *Adios,* Major Mitchell."

Chapter Sixteen

Jake Leach was still fretting over him and the other deputies not being allowed to go idling over to Rayburn's trading post with Matt Traxel. And it still puzzled him that Traxel had not just gone in force to Chase Donavan's place and simply killed the man. Hadn't it worked down at that plaza two days ago? He framed a stubbly-chinned smile just thinking about that Mexican woman he'd pleasured. His eyes as he rode swung to Harley Pierce. That was something too, Pierce grabbing that woman's baby by its heels and dashing its head against the log wall. When that had happened he'd almost thrown up over the woman spread-eagled under him.

"I tell you, Pierce, killing is better'n asking someone to clear out."

"I know, Jake, but we're getting paid to follow orders."

"But whose . . . MacGregor's or Traxel's?"

"What's the difference?" piped up Wyman. "From what I've heard this Donavan is one tough *hombre*. Once he hears our sermon about selling out, he'll probably order us off his land. Since there's three of us and one of him . . . why we'll just do what

Traxel is gonna do later."

"That cheers me up some. Been traveling along this river road for a considerable time . . . so just where in hell is his place?"

"You lift your eyes above your shoulders, Leach, you would'a spotted chimney smoke a spell ago. Another mile or so and we'll be there. By the way, what spiel from the Bible you gonna use this time?"

"You cotton to that do you, Pierce?"

"Reckon I do since you're the preacher of the damned." The hardcase cackled at what he'd said before thrusting his holstered .45 away from where it had been bouncing against his belly.

"My pa always cottoned to preaching from the New Testament . . . especially from the book of St. Luke." Jake Leach, pleasure brimming out of his sullen gray eyes, cleared his throat to make his Adam's apple bob against the dirty scarf encircling his thick neck. "From chapter one of that book, he did. 'To give light to them that sit in darkness and in the shadow of death.' Changed this next part—'to guide our guns once we unleather them.' Meaning it'll be Amen to Chase Donavan."

"You done missed your calling, Jake, danged if you didn't."

There was still in Rafael Martinez this deep well of apprehension brought about by what had happened just downriver. He knew that only cautious men lived for any great length of time out here. Though he wasn't sure of it, Rafael sensed the flames came from the plaza of Cristobal Baca. The man was old, almost ten years older than himself, and had long grown used to a peaceful existence

171

along the Purgatoire. But had not Hilario Madrid himself ridden down some weeks ago and discussed with Baca the need to keep one's guard up. What more could one do?

Now here he was alone at Chase Donavan's homestead, since Donavan and Felipe had driven the cattle into the breaks farther west of the river. Both of them — as was Jose from where'd he'd been keeping watch over the homestead of Jacob Purcell — were expected to return before nightfall. For company Rafael had a rifle loaned to him by Donavan; backing this up was an antique pistol he'd acquired many years ago down in New Mexico. But he was only adequate with both weapons. The big heavy skillet catching the heat of the stove would be the weapon he'd use if trouble came. Or the bone-handled knife Rafael honed after the tedious chores of day were over. But he hoped trouble would never come.

What had happened before was at best an elusive thing, at least to Rafael Martinez passing quietly through his late sixties. Three women had felt the power of his loins. The children he'd sired were long grown and scattered with the wind. Anymore he could scarcely recall any of their names, though one of them, Dominique, had visited his father two years ago. That he had survived three women was still a miracle to Rafael.

"Miracles," he said in a soft, wondering voice, "are a holy event. May such a miracle bring Cristobal Baca crossing my doorstep some day."

Sunken as he'd been in the recent tragedy of the burning and the more pleasant recalling of the past, Rafael only realized it had grown bitterly dark in the house of Chase Donavan when he set his mind

172

upon it. Allowing himself a chastening smile, he began turning slowly away from the meat frying in the skillet, only to be drawn short by a strange voice piercing in through the open front door.

"Hello the house!"

During the absence of the others Rafael had keep a careful watch to the east, the river and beyond to where travelers often ventured. That his uneasiness at being alone, and thoughts of the past, had served to drop his guard brought a frown to his seamed face.

Spearing a venison steak and flopping it over, Rafael muttered, "Probably it is some of these gringos wanting to water their horses. Always when I am busy."

On his way to the door Rafael reached to a wall peg for his sombrero and settled it over the few strands of white hair. He never went outside without donning the sombrero to hide his thinning hair, and he felt the hats shading presence gave him a certain dignity. Peering outside, he saw three cowhands, judging from their appearance, sitting their broncs on a patch of barren ground in front of the house. What brought him outside was that one of them was clasping a Bible in his gloved hand. Then Rafael Martinez saw something shining dully on the man's chest, and too late he realized it was a sheriff's badge.

"What was it Señor Donavan had said?" he asked himself.

"Well, greaser, just who owns this layout?" With the sun touching on the horizon Jake Leach was in no mood to ride any farther. Dusk was chow time, and by then a man should be holed up for the night. Pricking at his nostrils came the pleasant aroma of frying meat. This greaser probably had some hard liquor stashed away too.

"This is the *casa* of Señor Donavan," he said hesitantly.

"I get the feeling he's alone."

"So do I, Pierce. That was awful dumb of a man supposed to be so awful good with a gun."

They talked for a while amongst themselves as if the Mexican wasn't there. Wyman kept eying the gray gelding and the bay loafing in the corral. The horse he rode, a dun-colored bronc, could be trusted to buck every morning, then on the trail try to catch Wyman unawares. He'd gotten it cheap as a man could, taking the dun and almost a hundred dollars after bushwhacking a carpetbagger down in the Nations. With a savoring eye taking in the deep belly and long limbs of the gelding, the hardcase knew that rightfully he should have shot the dun back then too. At that moment he knew he had to have the gelding, and to get what he wanted meant only one thing — getting rid of the greaser. So in his sarcastic way the hardcase Wyman put his thoughts into words.

"Let's hang the greaser whilst we got a chance."

"You mean before Donavan shows up." Jake Leach tapped the leather-encased Bible against his saddle horn. "According to this here Bible — and what my pa taught me — don't hide under an oak tree during a lightning storm."

"What in tarnation is that supposed to mean?"

"Hellfire shall surely come upon us if us children don't take advantage of the situation."

"I get your drift, Jake," chortled Pierce. "Greaser, you're gonna get your *novenas* answered 'cause us angels of darkness are about to send you to the promised land." He laughed at the Mexican making a break for the house. Then he lashed his bronc ahead and rode at Rafael trying for the door. The muscular chest of the bronc struck Rafael Martinez in the back and threw him against the wall.

Somehow Rafael managed to block his forward momentum with his left arm, but he could feel the bones snap. The sombrero also cushioned some of the shock when his head encountered the wall, and dazed, he folded to the ground. What manner of men were these? Men who flaunted badges of the law yet could talk of hanging him?

"Hope you didn't kill him, Jake."

Swinging a leg over the saddle horn, Leach dropped to the ground and cast a scornful eye at the Mexican as he crossed the threshold and moved to the stove. "Damned if it ain't venison." He picked up the wooden-handled fork, speared out a hunk of meat, and chawed away as he paced back outside to find Wyman knotting a rope. Then he fastened a sardonic eye on the Mexican stirring about on the ground and moaning as he clutched his broken arm. "Greasers that old are hard to kill."

"Over there's a likely tree."

"Keep your breeches on, Wyman. You . . . greaser, tell us where Donavan is and we might let you skedaddle out of here."

This was another lie, Rafael knew. These were evil men, with much blood staining their evil hands. He stared up at Jake Leach holding a Bible in one hand and the piece of venison in the other, and into the man's waiting eyes. They were cruel eyes, the right having a mole over it and little tufts of hair sticking out. Rafael knew if he told them about Donavan they would hang him anyway.

"Señor . . . your *madre* most *ciertamente* was a whore."

Sudden anger flushing across his face, Leach came forward and kicked the Mexican in the ribs. Then he threw the fork away and reached down for his six-gun, thumbing the hammer back as it cleared the holster.

"Damn it, Jake, I want to hang the stupid bastard."

"What's the difference as long's he's dead."

"The difference is a bullet in the brain is over too quickly. Let him suffer at the end of my rope."

"Awright, hang the sonofabitch." Viciously he kicked the prone man again. Lowering the hammer on his gun, Leach shoved it into the holster. Now a smile touched upon his lips as he tapped the Bible. "I believe in the workings of this book, greaser. It says a man hung from a tree shall be accursed forever. So get to it, Wyman, get this greaser to sky-walking."

As his companions reached down for Rafael Martinez and brought him to his feet, Leach went over to a log pile and picked up an empty nail keg. He went ahead of the others to a lonely cottonwood and placed the keg under a low branch, and after doing that, he sent appreciative eyes beyond the house and westward where reddish streaks were pinking the underbellies of the few clouds. "A red sunset means this good weather'll continue. And I hope this don't take long 'cause I want some more of that venison."

Snaking the knotted rope around Rafael Martinez's quivering neck, they lifted him onto the keg and held him there as Wyman looped the rope around the branch and caught the loose end. Then

176

he drew the rope tight and grinned up at the Mexican. "Maybe you wanna tell me my ma was a whore too, greaser. . . ."

Above the pain eating at his broken arm Rafael could feel the dread of what was to come taking over. His body swayed through a spasm of weakness, but somehow he managed to say boldly, "A hinny . . . that's what your *madre* was!"

Puzzled, the hardcase inquired, "What the hell's that?"

Laughing at what the Mexican had said, Pierce spoke up. "You really want to know, Wyman? Okay. . . . the greaser claims your *madre* was the offspring of a stallion and a donkey." Now both Jake Leach and Pierce broke out laughing.

"I oughtta castrate you first, greaser!" Wyman tightened the slack in the rope as he began winding the end he held around the tree. He was the first one to be hit, a slug from Chase Donavan's rifle punching into his backbone.

More slugs came out of the darkness at the hardcases, but only Pierce was hit as Jake Leach dropped to the ground near the Mexican who'd fallen off the keg and simply lay there in shock.

"Jake, dammit . . . I'm hit . . . help me. . . ."

Leach didn't respond as he crawled over to the tree and managed to pull out his handgun and look about wildly. When a rifle boomed again, the slug from it punched into Pierce just lifting from the ground, and the hardcase dropped down dead.

"You! Drop that gun and stand up! Or the next bullet will drive your brains into that tree! Do it now, dammit!"

Jake Leach had no choice as another slug fanned past his cheekbone and buried itself deep in the cottonwood. "No more!" he shouted frantically and scrambled to his feet, somehow tossing his weapon away. Leach's Bible reposed over by Rafael gasping air into his lungs. This was a mistake coming here, was the hardcases forlorn thought as two horsemen materialized out of the gathering darkness and drew up close at hand. One of them, another Mexican, Leach noticed, dismounted quickly to tend to the old man. Now Jake Leach's gaze went to that of the man he'd come to see.

"You wasn't about," he began lamely. As Donavan closed in, Jake Leach was suddenly unnerved by the man's scarred face. Then Leach's jaws clamped shut as the badge was torn from his coat.

"You're no lawman," Chase said derisively. "Just another damned gunhand hired on by that cattle company."

"I . . . I don't know about that."

Chase threw over his shoulder. "How's Rafael?"

"His arm's broken—but otherwise he'll live."

"Felipe, sling that rope over that branch again."

"Now look, Donavan, we . . . we was only having some sport with the old greaser."

Chase lashed out with the barrel of his rifle and struck Jake Leach across the face, and as blood trickled from the hardcase's mouth, Chase said, "I lost my sense of humor a long time ago, sport." He grabbed Leach by the collar and brought him over to Felipe holding the rope. "Snug it around his neck."

They tipped the keg onto one end and made the hardcase stand on it, with Donavan taking the rope from the Mexican and removing just enough slack so that it snaked tight around Jake Leach's neck. Then he pulled it a little tighter.

"I know you work for Ian MacGregor," probed Chase. "That you were part of what happened just south of us. I can't hear you, sport!"

"I . . . damn, I work for MacGregor, awright."

"What part does Colonel James Ramsey play in this?" The branch creaked a little when he gave the rope a hard yank.

Gasping through his fear, Leach blurted out, "He made some deal with MacGregor."

"What kind of a deal?"

"That . . . that Ramsey was supposed to keep his men away from where we were operating. That's it, Donavan . . . I swear. . . ."

"Just as I thought," Chase pondered. "I figure you came here to burn me out or kill me. Where are the others?"

"It was just Wyman and Pierce and me coming here."

Chase propped a boot on the keg and gave it a shove.

"No! Not that! They're lazing over at that trading post—the one on the Santa Fe Trail—Matt Traxel and the others."

"What do you think, Felipe, should we hang him?"

But it was Rafael Martinez's voice that responded to Chase's question, not to determine the fate of Jake Leach, only to tell them horsemen were converging on the homestead. Chase's worried eyes turned toward the river, and in the uncertain light of early night, he could make out the saddles and regalia and uniforms of cavalrymen. Coming in with them was Jose. Upon reaching the house the soldiers drew rein, but continued toward the cottonwood upon glimpsing Jake Leach with a rope snugged around his neck. The soldiers fanned out to encircle the cottonwood, but it made no difference to Chase as he kept a firm grip on the hanging rope.

"I gather they came here next," ventured Major Mitchell. "Just want to say too, Mr. Donavan, it would probably cost me my commission if I let you hang that sonofabitch."

"Donavan . . . it's me . . . Sergeant Adamle."

"Hello . . . Adamle. Nice night for a ride."

"Yessir, guess it is. We came here a-purpose, sir."

"Chase—that name always struck me as being kind of different," said Mitchell. "I told you that back at Fort Chaffee."

When Chase released his grip on the rope, the hardcase toppled from the keg and fell heavily to the ground. For a while there'd been the feeling in Chase that he should know the major, but no question about that now. Mitchell had been lanker then, a lieutenant like him, with a sort of rebellious spirit matching Chase Donavan's. But just what had Burl Adamle told Major Mitchell? Perhaps Adamle was here to verify that he was indeed the same Lieutenant Chase Donavan wanted for murder and desertion. Chase wasn't hankering to spent any time in an army stockade.

"I see that dead man over there is wearing a badge," commented the major. "So were some of those who raided that plaza day before yesterday. What's your name?"

Jake Leach told the major as he came to his knees, and he added, "We were bona fide lawmen, Major, just doing our sworn duty."

"Leach, I'm placing you under arrest for murder. Tend to it, Sergeant Adamle." Mitchell swung down

180

and stepped toward Chase, whereupon he smiled and thrust out his hand. "Adamle told me the whole story, what happened down at Fort Randall. More importantly, I believe him." Then he shook Chase Donavan's hand.

"Don't know how to take this."

"You know, Chase, we could drop this here since the army considers you dead and buried. Which would mean that James Ramsey won't be punished for what he did. There's also the matter of honor, Chase, clearing your name."

"I've learned to live with that. But through Leach we can prove that Ramsey was taking orders from this cattle company. Ramsey is just as guilty of murder . . . down at that plaza . . . other places where people were gunned down. The problem is, Mitchell, will an army court-martial board believe the testimony of someone like Jake Leach."

"Sergeant Adamle has agreed to tell what he knows. Now we have you, Chase, along with some telegrams that were sent to Colonel Ramsey telling him where to send out patrols. Under the pressure of this evidence I'm certain Colonel Ramsey will say they were sent by Ian MacGregor."

"Ramsey's got to be stopped, no question about that. But right now I've got to tend to Rafael. You can overnight your horses in the corral, Mitchell. And we can probably come up with enough venison to feed everyone."

"One other thing, Donavan, how do you feel about going with us up to Fort Lyon?"

"When we're up there the rest of these marauders could ride in and burn me out. So my place is here until these men are captured. Then I'd be most pleased to make that ride upriver."

Chapter Seventeen

Shortly after Colonel James Ramsey had dispatched a patrol under command of Major K .C. Mitchell to scout that area to the southeast, Ramsey had gone the opposite way by stagecoach to Denver. The purpose of this trip had been to find out if Ian MacGregor had lived up to his promise by opening secret bank accounts in his name. The money was there, and Ramsey had taken a couple of thousand out and enjoyed his short visit in that mile high city. He'd divided his time between going to the opera and doing some gambling but spending a lot of time at a high-class brothel. He'd returned in a more relaxed frame of mind only to discover encamped at Fort Lyon an I. G. inspection team.

"So, Captain Brownell, it is your opinion that Colonel Ramsey is not guilty of dereliction of duty regarding where he sent his patrols. . . ."

"I have always had the utmost respect for Colonel Ramsey's judgement in these matters. We have all testified to that effect, sir. The fact remains our area of responsibility is quite large."

"Yes," agreed Colonel Reed Hamilton, "perhaps too large. The fact also remains, gentlemen, that up at division headquarters we have received a lot of complaints from those forced to leave their homes. Our duty first of all is to offer protection to these homesteaders. Despite the interference of the cattlemen."

Out of a clear sky, sunlight piercing down at newly-fallen snow came glaring into the hearing room and the worried eyes of James Ramsey. His concern was divided between these hearings and what was delaying Major Mitchell's patrol. They should have been back earlier in the week. Perhaps they had gone against his orders by scouting out the area around Trinidad. But even if they had, that was no concern of his. For there was no connection between him and what the men working for Ian MacGregor were doing, none at all.

On the other hand, the man presiding over these hearings, steely-haired Reed Hamilton, had a reputation for getting to the bottom of things. That suited him just fine, for he'd been running Fort Lyon with a firm hand. An inspection team always found a few things out of order, or Ramsey knew they weren't doing their job. But his officers with the exception of Major Mitchell backed him to a man. So perhaps it was fortunate that Mitchell wasn't here at the moment.

What he needed was time, until spring at the very least, and at least by then MacGregor's men and the big ranchers would have cleared the territory of most of the nesters and longtime squatters. His musings were disturbed by Colonel Hamilton saying the hearings would continue early tomorrow morning.

There came a scraping of boots as the assembled

officers rose, and Ramsey found Colonel Hamilton's eyes. "Reed, we all have our duties to perform. In a way I appreciate your coming here."

"Is that so?"

"Simply because this is one hard country to keep under control. What with all of these people coming in to rile up the cattlemen. I know it's just the encroachments of civilization . . . a fact a lot of people can't accept . . . which makes my job all the harder."

"One thing troubles me, Ramsey. Why haven't you stationed some of your troops down at Raton or Trinidad? Seems that's the logical thing to do."

"I had taken that under consideration," he lied suavely. "But the lawmen at both towns felt such a move wasn't necessary. Perhaps I should have overruled them."

"Doing just that will be one of my recommendations."

"Perhaps you'll join me for supper at the officer's club. . . ."

"There's still a meeting I'm having with my staff. See you in the morning, Ramsey."

Though he detected the coolness in Reed Hamilton's voice, James Ramsey nodded around a pleasant smile as he turned away and left the hearing room. He passed down a long corridor and entered his office to carefully close the door. Yesterday a wire had been delivered to him courtesy of Sergeant Major Hank Weaver. It had been sent from Trinidad; a dangerous move at this time, he thought angrily. After touching a match to the telegram, he'd ordered the sergeant major to send someone down to Old Las Animas and bring him a second wire. It was yesterday that he'd debated over destroying those other telegrams sent to him by Ian MacGregor. Though his eyes had strayed to the corner cabinet, he'd left the matter there.

"Colonel, you in there?"

"What now, Sergeant-Major?"

"That patrol of Mitchell's just rode in, sir. And that corporal I sent down to fetch your message just got here."

Shoving up from the desk, Ramsey veered to a window and gazed out at the troopers passing slowly along the parade grounds on their way to the stables. He continued on to the door and swung it open, to be handed an envelope by Hank Weaver.

"Might as well call it a day."

"Yessir." Weaver closed the door.

Hooking a finger under the closed flap of the envelope, Ramsey ripped it open and removed its contents. He read: "Do not understand your sending men to Trinidad. Need to confer with you. Suggest you come here."

"Just as I suspected!" blurted out James Ramsey as he crumbled the telegram up. "That damned maverick disobeyed my orders. I need more time . . . money. Dammit, I'm not going to let Mitchell or anybody else ruin this setup. But what . . . have Mitchell transferred to another post. . . ."

The sight of the telegram he held caused Ramsey to look over at where he'd stored the others sent to him by Ian McGregor. He knew the cabinet was locked, that he hadn't checked out its contents since receiving that last wire. Perhaps it was the presence of that I.G. team, or his anger over the major's blatant disregard of orders, but for some reason just looking at the cabinet brought a worried glimmer into his speculating eyes. He stepped past his desk to the corner and from his pocket fished out a small ring of keys. Suddenly he frowned, then reached for one of the door handles to have the door swing open.

"No."

Crouching down, he pulled the other door open and ignored everything but the leather pouch where he'd hidden the telegrams. A questing hand reached in and lifted out its contents. He saw a patch of yellow paper among the other documents and expelled a sigh of relief. But quickly he found only the one telegram, and James Ramsey broke out sweating.

That he was stunned by the unexpected loss of those telegrams showed in his wondering eyes and the way his hands were shaking. Think, dammit, figure this out! The only people who knew he'd been receiving these wires were the sergeant major and those soldiers he'd sent to fetch them from Old Las Animas. The telegraph operator down there, Chesley, could he have told someone here at Fort Lyon? No, it was either Weaver or —

"Wait a minute, why should whoever took the other telegram leave the last one I received from MacGregor. Who was it that the sergeant major sent down to Old Las Animas . . . yes, Sergeant Adamle. And what is there about Adamle that makes me think I've known him from before. His file should be in the orderly room."

186

He hurried into the adjoining room and to a wooden file cabinet, there to find Burl Adamle's personnel records in a lower drawer. Leafing through the military history of Sergeant Adamle, he discovered the man had served down at Fort Randall.

"Seven years ago? That means Adamle and I were there around the same time." He replaced the folder. Returning to his office, Ramsey paced the floor while trying to figure a way out of this. He didn't want to conduct a search of the barracks in an attempt to find those telegrams. Charges would have to be brought against Adamle. He could worry about that later. His first order of business was placing Adamle behind bars. After that an accident could be arranged. Meanwhile, he would have to destroy the one telegram Adamle hadn't stolen. And with the man's death, James Ramsey could deny any connection to the other wires. And afterward too, he would have to get together with Ian MacGregor and figure out a different way of passing messages up here to Fort Lyon.

Passing out of his dark office, Colonel Ramsey left the headquarters buildings and hurried to a stone building containing a small cell block and quarters for the duty officer. Much to his relief he found the duty officer was Captain Brownell. Just last week he had recommended Brownell be promoted to the rank of major, and Ramsey's presence now brought the captain pushing up from the table.

"Colonel, sir, is something wrong?"

"It seems a few military documents have been stolen from my office, Captain Brownell. I'll figure out the charges later. But now I'm ordering you to arrest Sergeant Burl Adamle."

"Sergeant Adamle doesn't seem the type, sir."

"Who knows what turns an enlisted man into a thief. I suggest, Captain, that you have an escort along when you arrest Adamle. Another thing, I want this kept quiet for the time being. Just don't want that inspection team getting wind of this."

"I understand perfectly, sir. We have to protect our own interests."

"This is one reason, Brownell, I recommended you be promoted. Your loyalty means a great deal to me. Carry on."

After reporting to his commanding officer the next morning Major K.C. Mitchell was not only reprimanded for disobeying orders but informed in no uncertain terms that he would be transferred.

"My opinion is that the army erred in giving you a commission."

"I'm awful sorry about that, sir."

"Mitchell, your insolence becomes you."

Earlier this morning the sergeant major had dropped by Mitchell's quarters to tell him that Burl Adamle was taking his ease in the post stockade. So it was fairly evident to him that the colonel had discovered those telegrams sent to him by MacGregor were missing. He'd learned from Adamle that after Chase Donavan had been arrested and placed behind bars down at Fort Randall an attempt had been made on Donavan's life. Staring back at a man he'd learn to hate, K.C. Mitchell knew that if he asked why Sergeant Adamle had been arrested it would tip Ramsey off to his involvement in this. But at the moment Burl Adamle was as good as dead unless something was done to spring him from the stockade.

"In my report, sir, I made it clear that those Mexicans living along the Purgatoire were killed by white men and not Utes."

"Did I say that Indians killed these people?" Ramsey said savagely.

"Colonel, you didn't say much of anything."

"Get out of here you insolent bastard. And remember, Mitchell, don't leave the post."

"Does this mean I'm confined to quarters—"

"Get out!"

In passing through the orderly room Major Mitchell motioned for the sergeant major to follow him outside. Then both men fell into step, with Mitchell not saying anything until they were screened by an adjoining building. "Adamle's life could be in danger."

"Just what's going on sir?"

"Hank, we've served together through good and bad . . . before they sent Ramsey out here. Just want to say that before long all hell is gonna break loose. So just how thick are you with the colonel?"

"Easy, K.C., er, Major Mitchell, around him I just obey orders. Just what did you find out on this patrol?"

"That a lot of killing is being done," he said grimly. "That our esteemed colonel is mixed up in it."

"Damn, I hate to hear it when an officer goes

189

bad. An enlisted man, well, the landed gentry and officers expect it of him. But the officers serving under Ramsey are a clannish bunch."

"Except me being the black sheep hereabouts. Who's heading up this I.G. inspection team?"

"Colonel Hamilton."

"Reed Hamilton?"

"Yup."

"He's the one turned me from a sergeant into a shave-tailed wonder. That was a few hard years ago, Hank. The only way I can save Adamle's skin is to tell what I know to Colonel Hamilton."

"I know Ramsey had Adamle arrested—something about Adamle stealing some papers—but murder, that's letting in too much wind."

"Ramsey committed murder before, Hank. Down in Texas. But keep this to your lonesome, Sergeant Major, or Adamle might not see another sunrise."

"Back in the wild days you were quite an Indian fighter. Reason I wrangled you that commission. Grab a chair, K.C., and tell me what this is all about. Cigar?"

"Don't mind if I do, Colonel Hamilton." Major Mitchell pulled a chair away from the table and sat down across from the colonel, whose probing gray eyes took in Mitchell's ruddy skin and the worried gaze as they exchanged glances.

"I understand you just came back from a patrol."

"I did, sir. Found out why a lot of homesteaders are pulling out." In crisp words he narrated coming in too late to save those at the plaza.

"A horrible thing to happen. These Mexicans are fine people."

"Sir, here's the dry bones of why I'm here. If the proper orders would have been issued, these killings wouldn't have happened."

"Just what are you accusing Colonel Ramsey of doing . . . or not doing? And remember, K.C., old friends or not I want proof of any accusations."

"The charge against James Ramsey is murder!"

Colonel Hamilton let a thoughtful halo of smoke pass through his lips as the man across the table pulled out of an inner coat pocket several telegrams. These were placed on the table. Mitchell looked at them as he formulated his thoughts. He began by telling of how he had been brought to Lieutenant Chase Donavan by Adamle, and of their connection to events long ago at Fort Randall, that both men would testify in a military court of law as to Colonel James Ramsey's past misdeeds. And more currently, he tied in the telegrams with Ian MacGregor and his Prairie Cattle Company, thus connecting them to these recent killings.

"So you can see, sir, Sergeant Adamle might be taken out by Ramsey. Because Ramsey can't afford to have Adamle testify."

"K.C., this is one helluva story."

"Every word is gospel, sir. When Sergeant Adamle first came to me and showed me these telegrams . . . thought the man was just liquored up . . . but he proved me otherwise. Ramsey doesn't know that Chase Donavan is alive."

"That should prove interesting when these two get together. K.C., I have to digest this . . . slowly . . .

damned slowly." Hamilton picked up the telegrams and shuffled through them.

"There's one way to find Ramsey out, Colonel Hamilton, along with maybe saving Sergeant Adamle's life."

"Try it on me."

"Colonel, this is the way I got it figured. . . ."

Glancing up from the book he'd been reading, Lieutenant Dave Martin peered up at the wall clock and said quietly, "Almost eleven—time to make my rounds."

He didn't mind being duty officer, for it gave him quiet moments like this to read classics or study military tactics. Usually the wind would be yowling out of the Rockies, but tonight a brooding silence seemed to hang over Fort Lyon. Maybe, he pondered, because that inspection team was still here. He drank what little coffee there was left in his cup, and, rising, reached over for his military overcoat. As he slipped into the coat, he glanced again at the clock, impatience ruffling up his smooth brow.

"What's keeping Corporal Littleton? Can't make my rounds until someone is here to watch the prisoner."

Another ten minutes found the lieutenant's patience growing thin, and somewhat edgily he opened the door, stepped out into the cold night air and looked anxiously toward the barracks housing the enlisted men. About the only thing he could do now was go and roust Corporal Littleton out of his bunk along with putting the man on report. And he hurried that way. Then it happened, a dark shadow easing out from the side of the stone building and clubbing Lieutenant Martin from behind. The ambusher caught Martin as he was falling and dragged the unconscious man along the side wall. A short distance away lay the still form of Corporal Littleton.

Colonel James Ramsey hurried out and looked around nervously before pacing inside and easing the door shut. He could have killed both the corporal and the lieutenant, but his target was Burl Adamle. The door running back to the cells was open, and by lantern light he could see that Adamle was stretched out on a cot in the second cell to his left. He'd brought along a knife, and would use this to slit his intended victim's throat. He found the key to the cells on a wall hook. Silently he padded back among the cells, unlocked the door and left the key in the lock while slipping into the cell and staring down at Adamle bundled up snugly in his blankets. Ramsey's eyes drifted to the empty bunk to Adamle's right and the pillow on it.

"Why not use my gun . . . since that pillow will muffle any sound it makes. That way I won't get any blood on myself."

He reached for the pillow, then turned back to the other bunk. There was just enough light in the cell to make out Adamle's head almost hidden under the blankets but snugged down on a pillow. Gently he placed the barrel of his revolver against the blanket and quickly covered it with the pillow. The revolver bucked in his hand as its muffled report barely carried out of the cell window.

"There . . . that takes care of any past encumbrances." A smile drove away some of his nervousness as he turned away from the bunk.

Then Colonel James Ramsey stopped dead in his tracks as someone said harshly, "Drop it, Ramsey!"

"What the—" He stared in disbelief at the men flooding in from the duty officer's room and opposite through a rear door.

"Don't do anything foolish, Ramsey. All you killed tonight was some blankets made to look like someone has been sleeping there. But what you just did proves you committed murder down at Fort Randall. No . . . Ramsey—"

Major K.C. Mitchell and those with him flinched away from the sight of James Ramsey placing the barrel of his gun to his temple and pulling the trigger. This time the sound of Colonel Ramsey's service revolver carried well away from the post stockade. As blood and brains splashed onto the stone wall, the commandant of Fort Lyon fell lifelessly onto the cot and what he'd thought was the body of Burl Adamle.

After a while Major Mitchell said sadly, "I know a man who was fixing to meet up with the colonel."

To his left another colonel, Reed Hamilton, said, "I expect that'll be a man named Donavan. Mitchell, seems its gonna be boots and saddles in the morning. This time we'll send two companies. You'll be in charge."

"Obliged, sir. Didn't think Ramsey had enough nerve to kill himself."

"I'd say it was lack of courage and fortitude that killed the man."

"Your point of view sounds a lot better, sir, a helluva lot better."

Chapter Eighteen

The dying remnants of a hurricane had sent storm clouds spreading up through Texas and down along the Purgatoire. Most of the snow had melted, though patches still lay in the hollows and ravines spreading away from the river which had risen considerably. For the last couple of days there'd been scattered showers from clouds twisting away to the north.

"I expect," said Chase, "this reminds you of Mexico."

Jose Cardenas shrugged as he turned an eye to the distant rumble of thunder. "At least we don't have snow."

"What I'm worried about is this weather fetching in twisters."

"Eastward on the plains maybe," said Cardenas. "Very few of them touch down here. And I have been here over twenty years. But I don't know, the way these clouds are coming in."

A day after the cavalry patrol had trailed out for Fort Lyon, Chase had sent Felipe and Rafael Martinez back to their homes. Though both men were reluctant to go, with Rafael saying he could still get in a whack or two with his skillet, it was Chase's feeling they would be safer up north at the plaza.

Jake Leach had talked freely after he realized the army had no intention of letting him go, along with saying he'd testify against Ian MacGregor. But Leach had been reluctant to volunteer any information about gunfighter Matt Traxel, that is, until Chase informed Leach he still had his hanging rope. Then out of the hardcase came a wordslide detailing how Traxel operated.

From this Chase had determined that the two of them wouldn't stand a chance against all of that firepower. Neither would Jacob Purcell and his family. So after sending Felipe and Rafael on their way, Chase put up a couple of grave markers adorned with the hats of the dead hardcases and their monikers over their resting places. This was almost certain to rile up a prideful killer like Matt Traxel. Later that same day, and the next, he and Cardenas had ridden onto the crest of a butte and kept watch in the hopes they could spot those marauders.

"We sure left a plain enough trail for them banditos to follow," Jose said.

"I'm betting they'll be coming after us," Donavan replied.

"For sure, Señor Donavan, they'll burn down your buildings first."

"That's another gamble, Jose. What bothers me now is how stubborn Jacob can be. I hope we can talk him into going with us up to Hilario's."

"Surely he must realize the danger from these banditos."

"A man can always rebuild. But Jacob doesn't see things the same as me."

197

Stretching to their left but several rods away was the river. At this point the road meandered off to the east to avoid a hill. Rainwater had settled in ruts; but the ground was hard, and Chase knew it wouldn't soak in but form ice when the weather cooled down again. The wind came at their backs to help push them along. As he rode, Chase let thoughts of Raven push away how he felt about leaving his homestead at the mercy of these men.

Jose brought his horse sideways and stared along their backtrail for a long minute, then he said, "They are back there."

"Trailing us?" Chase swung his loping horse around.

"Not yet . . . but back there."

"Maybe this weather is spooking you."

"This has happened to me before . . . when I was tracking a mountain lion. Suddenly I comprehended the cat was tracking me. Then there it was. But I managed to get in a lucky shot. They are back there—perhaps at your homestead."

At a nod from Chase they brought their horses away from the road and let them pick their own way up the hill. Here the wind came at them as though they had opened a door, but warming and laden with moisture. Chase drank from his canteen as his bronc nibbled at short grass growing around the many rocks.

"Can that be a low cloud or smoke?"

"Damn, it's smoke, Jose. Coming from my place. All that work for nothing." The skin on his face tightened, and Chase wished now that he had stayed put. Calming down, he added, "Timber comes cheap out here. How long do you figure before they pick up our trail?"

"What is it . . . around the middle of the afternoon? They won't like finding only two graves. They'll want to find the third one, Leach. And you, Señor Donavan, to avenge the deaths of the others. They'll come hard."

"We've got a couple of hours' headstart. And Jacob's place isn't more'n a mile or two away. At least we've got two hours. Vamoosing time, Jose."

Everytime he came over here Chase had an appreciative eye for the way Jacob Purcell had laid out his buildings. To the north about a quarter of a mile, a low ridgeline gave the buildings some protection from the prevailing northerly winds, as did the few trees, although the homesteader had planted a double row of fir seedlings. The foundation for the barn Jacob hoped to put up lay northeast of the house, while the spacious log house faced the south. The north wall of the house contained a pair of recessed windows, and on the sloping roof a dormer window also faced that way. A lot of times Jacob's son would cut up into the attic and gaze out that window at the hazy mountains, and Chase envied him for being in that daydreaming age.

"It's still the shank of the afternoon," commented Chase as he brought his horse past a shed. At this time of day Jacob could always be found sawing or hammering away at some kind of construction work in his attempt to get the barn going before winter really set in.

"The horse he rides is in the corral," said Jose. He drew up alongside Chase, and both men dismounted by the corral to tie their reins to a pole.

"Chase, I'm so glad you're here," Clara greeted.

He swung toward Clara Purcell hurrying out of the front door while wiping her hands on her dark blue apron. But even at this distance he could see the worried set to her oval face.

"Howdy boys," she called out. "Jacob's inside tending to one of our yonkers. At first we thought Billy just had dropsy. But it's worse than that. But land sakes, do come in, Chase, Jose."

"Clara, I hope Billy is well enough to leave here."

"Leave? He's . . . got scarlet fever. Why, is something wrong?"

"Those men who've been doing all this killing have hit my place. It could be they'll be here next."

"But, Chase, we can't leave! Not with Billy laid up like this. He's awful bad . . . tried giving him some medication to get the fever down . . . and done some praying."

"Sometimes prayers aren't answered," Jose said hesitantly. "It was scarlet fever that killed my two little ones. Other children died too. But we did save most of them. You must rub your son from head to toe with a piece of fat bacon, every morning and night. Do you have any belladonna or perhaps some sweet spirits of nitre?"

"Please, Jose, if you would help us. . . ." She went ahead of them into the house. "We've been using spirits of nitre."

"*Si*, that will help. He must be sweated. If not, what he has will bring on other diseases."

200

Jacob Purcell came out of the bedroom and threw them a harried glance as he passed into the kitchen. "You boys came at a bad time."

"Seems that way," replied Chase. Removing his hat, he dropped it onto a hard-backed chair and gave the Purcell's other son a curt smile. "Sorry to hear your brother's under the weather."

David Purcell was towheaded and had the soft green eyes of his mother. The homespun shirt and corduroy trousers hung loosely on his lank frame. A week ago the boy had celebrated his twelfth birthday. There was this hankering in him to be like Chase Donavan, or like that mountain man who'd passed through a month ago. He had a keen eye for something that was amiss, and he knew that only trouble had brought Donavan this way. He allowed a tentative smile to lift the edges of his mouth.

"Billy's got something bad, Mr. Donavan."

"You've been doing much riding lately?"

"When Pa lets me . . . or I can sneak off by my lonesome."

"Suppose someday you'll want to be a cowboy."

"Maybe," David Purcell grinned.

Nodding, Chase took Jose aside and murmured softly, "Ride out a couple of miles and keep watch for those killers. It just might be they'll bypass this place or head back to Trinidad."

"I hope you're right, Donavan." Jose Cardenas shouldered through the door and found his horse.

Chase went into the kitchen and said to Jacob Purcell slumped at the table, "There's a possibility, Jacob, we might have to pull out of here in a hurry. Because right now my place has been set afire." He glanced at Sarah hanging on every word as she placed a coffee cup before him. He wrapped a hand around the cup, then took a sip of the chicory coffee. Now Chase told them how two men came to be buried at his homestead and the army taking a third man up to Fort Lyons. "Matt Traxel and the rest of them are gunfighters."

"Why didn't those soldiers stick around and help us out?"

"They were under orders to report back. But I've got Major Mitchell's promise they'll be coming down again. The important thing now, Jacob, is to realize these hardcases mean business. No matter how you feel about this place it won't help if you're dead."

Sarah Purcell said, "It makes no difference, Chase, because we can't leave because of Billy. Look at it out there . . . it's raining. Take him out in that and he'll die."

"We can't risk that," Chase agreed. "If they come, this is where we'll have to make a stand. You have those two old rifles—"

"Those," Jacob responded, "and the Winchester I bought. Along with plenty of bullets. Been doing some practicing with it when these troubles began. Can't say I'm all that good, Chase, but if these men do come I hope to give a good account of myself."

"We can't afford to send Cardenas up to bring help . . . up to Hilario's
plaza. But there's your boy David."

"He's only twelve. . . ."

"I know, Clara. But we've got no other options. It's around seven miles."

"Jacob," she said, "must we risk our son's life. Perhaps these outlaws will leave us alone."

But Clara Purcell's hopes were shattered when through the kitchen window they glimpsed Jose Cardenas coming in at a gallop. Dismounting at a run, he came in the kitchen door. "A bunch of them about four miles out and heading this way."

"That cuts it," Chase told them. "Jose, you help these folks close the window shutters while I tend to your horse. David can take my horse." He hurried into the other room to find that David Purcell had been eavesdropping by the open doorway. "Well, son, you know what needs to be done."

"I guess I just take the river road up there." He ran over and got his hat and coat and went outside with Chase.

"Seven miles up there. The road will dip toward the river to avoid a hill marked by a big oak tree that was struck by lightning. When you see that, cut down toward the river and you'll find a crossing. Tell Madrid what the situation is . . . that we need every man he can muster." At his horse, he helped the boy into the saddle and thrust the reins into his small hands. He removed his rifle from the saddle boot. "Go to it, son."

As David Purcell brought the horse to the north along a dry wash, Chase hurried over and grabbed the ground-hitched reins and brought Jose's horse over to the corral. He left the horse with the others and went back into the house. He'd spotted the hardcases just swinging off the river road. A long mile would bring them here.

Jose said, "We've taken the mattress of the boy's

bed and placed it on the floor. The boy should be safer there. How do you want to work this?"

"Let them fire the first shot," ventured Jacob.

"They'll know we're here. That shed fronting onto the house—a good place to catch them in a cross-fire."

"I'll go."

"Nope, I suggested it, Jose. I have a notion they'll send in one or two to try and palaver with you, Jacob. Just don't venture out past the front porch, as these men can't be trusted." He gave Jacob a reassuring pat on the shoulder and let himself out the front door. The house screened him from the hardcases coming in from the west. Inside the shed, he levered a shell into the breech of his Winchester while peering out through a small window.

Perhaps ten minutes later a signal from Jose standing by a front window alerted Chase to the presence of the outlaws, and then three of them swung their horses around the corner of the house and drew up cautiously. By his count there were about twenty of them. The others would be spreading out as these three drew the attention of those defending the house.

"What do you want?" Jacob yelled.

"Come out where we can see you, Purcell."

The door came ajar. "How'd you know my name?"

"Over at the county courthouse is how. That's better. Nice layout you've got here. But too bad you built it on land belonging to the Prairie Cattle Company."

"That's not what they told me over at the court-

204

house!"

"Makes no difference what they told you, Purcell. I'm making you a once and final offer for these buildings of one hundred dollars."

"Damn you thieving—" Jacob Purcell stepped over the threshold and glared back at the man who'd been spokesman for the hardcases. "You are nothing more or less than thieves and murderers."

From his vantage place in the shed, Chase could see another hardcase slowly inching out a Smith Wesson. The way he sat his saddle, his gunhand was shielded from Jacob, whose own anger blinded him to the danger he was facing. When the hardcase thumbed back the hammer as he brought up his weapon, Chase fired a slug that ripped into the man's head.

"What the—?" One hardcase reached for his six-gun as he swung his horse around while the other simply jabbed spurs into the flanks of his horse and headed for the corner of the house.

Almost at the same instant that Chase had pulled the trigger the gunhand was levering the action on his Winchester. The hardcase fired at the door of the shed and then at the window, to have a slug splinter into the wall near Chase's head. Chase pumped two slugs at the horseman and watched the man tumble out of the saddle. The bronc reared, and when it came down a front hoof landed on the outlaw's head. Then, in its fear at what had taken place, the horse galloped away. Chase swung the door open and broke for the house.

Pow-Pow-Pow

While two slugs tucked at his clothing a third

found Chase's left arm, and though he broke stride, he managed to rush through the door followed by angry bullets pounding at the door and wall. He slammed the door shut as Jose Cardenas dropped the wooden door brace across the supports to either side. "You hit bad?"

"Had toothaches that were worse than this."

"For sure they've got us cornered," Jacob called out as he came in from the kitchen. "Quite a bunch of them. Can you imagine them offering me a hundred dollars for my place."

"What they wanted, Jacob, was to see how many guns we had. Glad it cost them two men." Chase glanced around at the shuttered windows and thick doors as he tried ripping his shirt sleeve away from the bullet wound. "If our ammo doesn't give out, we can hold them off."

"The boy . . . I hope he gets to Hilario," Jose commented.

"David's got grit," Jacob Purcell said. "That slug still in there?"

"Punched on through."

"I'll heat some more water, Chase. And there's some whiskey to sterilize that wound."

Chase felt better when the wound had been tended to by Clara Purcell and a bandage covered it. His inquiries about their son brought the response that Billy seemed to be resting comfortably. For some time now the marauders hadn't fired at the house, though when they had, a couple of errant bullets had wormed past the shutters and decorated the inner walls. Earlier, too, Jose had climbed up into the attic and utilized the dormer window.

206

He'd winged one man, plugged another in the upper chests, and once again his voice came down the wall ladder.

"Smoke is coming from one of your sheds!"

"A hard price to pay, Jacob," said Chase.

"What about you? They burned you out."

"Could have been worse."

"That's something to smile about," Jacob said bitterly. "Once it gets dark they'll move in . . . try to set fire to the house."

"With this rain it'll be hard. Won't be dark for another three hours." He snaked a glance out of the shuttered window in the direction of the corral. The horses were still there, and Chase realized the marauders hadn't moved them in the hope those holed up in the house would try and break out. The clouds slipping past now, darker than they'd been this morning, were twisting about and formless so at times Chase couldn't tell in which direction they intended going. Weather like this could last for a while, but if it dumped rain on this sparse land the discomfort of having it could be endured.

He stepped toward the bedroom as Clara Purcell rose from where she'd been tending to her son, and he said, "Wish I could sleep like that."

"Billy seems to be a little better since I tried steaming out some of the fever. I'm sorry you got hurt, Chase."

"Just a nick." He stepped into the small bedroom and nodded at the shuttered window. "You know, what's happened has sure whet my appetite. Now, Mrs. Purcell"—he dragged a chair over by the window—"sit down and take your ease for a spell 'cause

I'm going to whip some chow together."

She forced a hesitant laugh. "Haven't eaten all day. Sounds like a good idea. And I sure could rest my feet."

After she eased onto the chair, Chase set the rifle against the wall and said, "I've still got my six-gun. You still keep your taters in that bin by the cupboard?"

"Still do . . . but as I remember hearing it from your missus, you're one terrible cook."

"Man's got to learn, ma'am."

"With that wound you're nothing but a one-armed cook, Mr. Donavan. But go ahead . . . if it'll set your mind at ease. Bacon's hanging in the pantry."

Upon entering the kitchen Chase found Jacob Purcell gazing out a crack in a window at his burning shed. The buffeting wind was tossing the flames about. And it had stopped raining. As they watched for a while, both of them noticed it was becoming shadowy out.

"David's been gone about two hours," Jacob said worriedly.

"Should be up there."

Suddenly Chase flinched away as bullets began thudding into the kitchen door and the window, and while Chase remained in the kitchen, Purcell hurried into the living room and made for his rifle propped by a window.

"You, in the house!"

Peering out of a kitchen window Chase could make out the vague outline of a man lurking by the shed, and he held his fire. From the description given him by Jake Leach, the man who'd called out

208

could only be Matt Traxel. He didn't seem as tall as in Leach's telling, and Traxel's hat was sogged out of shape from the rain while a yellow slicker encased the man's stout frame.

"Jacob Purcell," the gunfighter shouted again, "there's no way in hell you're gonna get out of this. We've got plenty of bullets and all the time in the world. And . . . Donavan, if things were different I'd enjoy matching draws. But you killed three of my men. You're dangerous, Donavan, so you can burn with the other sodbusters in there."

Chase brought up his six-gun just as the gunfighter slipped behind the shed. "Damn him," he said, turning to look at Jacob coming into the kitchen.

"What do you think, Chase? Should we try and break out of here?"

"That's what Traxel wants. We've got a chance as long as we stay in here. You built pretty good . . . and this rain has wet down the walls and roof."

Jose Cardenas slipped down from the attic and held his hands over the stove to warm them as he said worriedly, "Señor Purcell, some of these banditos have hitched up your wagon. Lost sight of it when they drove it behind some trees."

"I've got a sizable woodpile out that way."

"It's getting dark out," Chase said. "I figure they'll load some wood on that wagon and then set fire to it. Try to run it against the house to set it afire."

"What about the boy?" Jose asked.

"If he made it up to the plaza, Jose, help should be on the way." Chase forced a smile. "Coffee's fresh, boys."

209

"*Sí*, we are still alive. Your boy, Señor Purcell, is very brave. But all the same, I shall say a silent prayer for him . . . and for us."

As Jose Cardenas stepped to the table and reached for a cup, the hardcases opened up on the house. A few bullets punched through the kitchen windows and struck the walls, with one ricocheting away from the cast iron stove and clipping away Jacob Purcell's right earlobe. But the homesteader barely paused as he followed Chase into the living room, with Jose trailing to crouch by a north window.

"Clara, keep down in there."

"I'm froze to the floorboards, Jacob. Will they ever give up?"

"Don't fret now," he said tautly.

"There's been some lightning?" questioned Jose. "But . . . what is this . . .?"

Chase wrenched one of the shutters open and shouted, "They've set that wagon on fire!"

What he saw careening past the shed were two horses hitched to the wagon being driven by a man balancing himself on the wagon tongue and traces. The hardcase kept lashing his reins at horses frightened by the burning wagon they were pulling. The horses shielded the hardcase from Chase's gun even as the others outside caught sight of Chase Donavan and began concentrating their firepower on the open window. In desperation he fired at the horses, but suddenly they veered aside as the man sawing at the reins had managed to pull the connecting pin from the wagon tongue. Chase felt a slug scour alongside his cheekbone as the burning wagon came

210

trundling straight for the front door.

"Get back!" he warned. Spinning away from the window, he grabbed Jacob's arm and pulled him deeper into the living room.

The runaway wagon struck the lower part of the porch and bounced into the air, causing it to pitch most of its burning cargo at the walls of the house, with the wagon coming on to break open the door. Chase shoved the homesteader and his family toward the bedroom, then he motioned Jose over to him.

"Sorry I got you into this."

"By my own *acuerdo* I am here."

"They'll be coming in . . . fast and wanting to kill." Chase gripped Jose Cardenas' arm and managed to smile back. Then he heard a gun cutting loose as Jose stiffened from the impact of being hit, and only now did Chase see the broken shutter in the kitchen.

"Señor Chase . . . I—" Jose Cardenas pirouetted around on weakened legs in the direction of the kitchen.

"Damn you!" Chase emptied his gun at the man who'd just gunned down Cardenas. Even as the hardcase folded over the windowsill, others of his killing breed were converging on the front door. Chase knew that it was just a matter of time before the fire or these murderers killed all of them. He turned to Jose, who'd crumbled to his knees, and then the back door seemed to give as something hard punched into it. With flames engulfing the front door, Chase knew they were trapped. Quickly he reloaded his six-gun and thrust it into his holster

211

as he picked up Jose's rifle. Reflexively he fired at a man framing himself in the open kitchen window, levered the rifle, then began firing at the kitchen door as he hurried toward it. The angry scream of a marauder getting hit pierced through the shattered door panes . . . and then something else . . . a sound from out of Chase Donavan's past.

Those assaulting the house also heard the call of a bugler, and suddenly they were fleeing away from the brightness of the flames eating at the house and making for their horses. They soon found themselves fighting a mixture of cavalrymen under the command of Major K.C. Mitchell and men from Hilario Madrid's plaza. Chase managed to open the back door. He went outside looking for a marauder to vent his rage on, but the firefight was taking place beyond the corral and sheds; and then Jacob Purcell came to stand by Chase.

"It's raining harder," Chase said. "Seems to be putting out the fire. But we'd better get some of those burning logs away from the front door."

"Your arm?"

"I've got one good arm, Jacob, and two sound legs. Come on."

They hurried around and laid their weapons aside before yanking the few burning logs away from the house. Even as they struggled to save the house, out of the darkness came Madrid and at least a dozen others from his plaza. Under Madrid's direction they formed a bucket brigade extending the short distance from the well to the front of the house, and this combined with the steady rain put out the flames.

"Hold your fire!" yelled Major Mitchell as he appeared with Sergeant Burl Adamle a short distance behind. "We killed most of them, Chase. But one or two got away."

"Did you kill Matt Traxel?"

"Can't be sure."

"Lets go take a look," Chase said grimly.

Some of the marauders had been wounded, but scattered about in the trees where they'd left their horses were several bodies. Even in the dim light of night Chase knew that Matt Traxel had gotten away. Traxel would figure it this way . . . that the soldiers coming in meant Colonel Ramsey had doublecrossed them . . . and so the gunfighter would make tracks for Trinidad to have a showdown with Ian MacGregor.

"Trinidad . . . Raven is there."

Matt Traxel or even MacGregor could take out their anger on his wife and son, and Chase swung around and hurried toward the buildings. This time lamps had been lighted, and he spotted his horse tethered out front. When he reached to untie the reins, David Purcell and his father appeared in the battered and charred door frame.

"Nice work, David."

"When I got up there, Mr. Donavan, the army was just riding in."

"Jose — seems he'll pull through. You heading someplace?" Jacob asked.

Chase Donavan settled onto the saddle. "Trinidad."

"That's right, Raven is there."

"If she's still alive."

Spurring the horse over, Chase reached for the Winchester propped against the wall and thrust it into the leather scabbard. Then he loped away into the stormy night, only to have Major Mitchell come ghosting up.

"I guess you're headed for Trinidad. Can't say as I blame you, Donavan. But from here on in this is army business."

"The army and I called it quits a long time ago."

"Donavan, the man who drummed you out of the army is dead. Ramsey killed himself up at Fort Lyon. And from the testimony given by Sergeant Adamle, your record has been cleared."

"Can't say I'll mourn the colonel's passing. But there's others like him down at Trinidad. Meaning I can't take the chance they'll try to get even with me by going after my family."

At a lope Chase Donavan headed his bronc into the stormy night.

Chapter Nineteen

The horse began going lame where the river made a wide slash to the west. For a while Chase tried holding it at a canter, knowing that he should have left his horse at Jacob's and switched to a fresh mount. He swung down at times and brought the horse along at a walk, with each step he took upon the soggy river road jarring at his wound.

"You and me, hoss, are two cripples looking for a place to die."

Sometimes on the river road as he stared ahead at the ground, he could make out hoofmarks left by three horsemen who'd passed this way not over an hour or two ago.

"Traxel was one of them."

There was this hope in Chase that the gunfighter and his cronies, and even Ian MacGregor, would realize the game was over and pull out of Trinidad. Maybe Matt Traxel would. But the Scotsman had too much invested out here.

"Never could cotton to a man adorned with both suspenders and a belt. Nope, hoss, MacGregor's not the kind to leave a plugged nickel behind . . . much less all the land he's latched on to."

Rainwater trickling off the brim of Chase's hat

sated his thirst when he drew it into his mouth. But it was a cold rain, letting up at times, then pouring again out of clouds he glimpsed when lightning brightened up the darkness. By his reckonings Trinidad was still another four miles to the south. Almost there, was Chase's reviving thought. He sought the saddle but brought his horse along slowly, for it had just occurred to him that he could see a shade farther along the road peeling wetly to the south now. He could make out the river glinting off to the west and realized he'd gone around that big bend. Then a familiar landmark revealed itself, an abandoned sodhouse sunk deep in the ground. Easing down, Chase led his hobbling bronc in through the fringes of the cowtown.

A few lights sparkled out of windows where early risers were up and about. Other than this Trinidad still slumbered on in the afterglow of night. Just ahead lay Main Street and probably the men he was after, but that could wait as Chase padded tiredly down a sidestreet. He soon found the house of Armando Sanchez hidden behind an adobe wall. Leaving the horse in the courtyard, he stepped under the overhanging porch and lifted a weary hand to remove his hat and slap it against his yellow rain slicker to dry it some. Then it struck him, the way the shadows were lifting, Raven was always up long before this. He peered in a dark window, but could detect no light reflecting into the living room from the kitchen. He passed along a side wall and found the back door; it stood open with the broken lock bringing Chase inside.

"Anybody here? Sanchez? Raven?"

He found the boy first, Jesse Keepseagle, up by the front door. The killers had used a knife, and Chase grimaced away from the bloody gash tracking across the boy's throat.

"Jesse, damn . . . it's my fault, son." From where he crouched Chase reached over for a round knitted floor rug and covered the boy.

He came erect and hurried along a narrow hallway. The first bedroom was Raven's, but it was empty, as was the second. In the remaining bedroom he came upon the bodies of Armando Sanchez and his wife.

"The bastards used knifes." Calmly, he told himself, as Chase placed a hand upon the face of the woman to find she was still warm. "They were killed no more'n an hour ago."

This time he went out the front door and sought his saddle. "Just a little farther, hoss." As he reined around, Chase had to fight back a despairing tear forming in his eye. But that moment of weakness fled from the terrible wrath that stoned his face. MacGregor . . . had a suite at the Colorado Hotel . . . and the men who did this would also be there.

Chase brought his walking horse onto Main Street just beginning to awaken to a new day. It was then he unlimbered the Winchester. Every so often thunder laid its drumming sound over the town, this mixed with heavy rainwater and lightning flaring. Up ahead on the next block he could see the upper reaches of the hotel and some horses tethered out front, with two men taking their ease by the horses. And as Chase worked the lever on his rifle, he watched Matt Traxel step around the far

217

corner of the hotel and climb aboard his horse. Chase urged his bronc into a lope as one of the gunhands chanced to look his way, and Chase brought the rifle to his shoulder and fired just as the man called out a warning to his companions.

He downed the first hardcase and struck the horse of the second. Traxel snapped off a lonely shot and disappeared around the corner, leaving Chase to confront one of the hardcases. The bearded gunhand stepped away from his falling horse and began fanning bullets at Chase riding low over the shoulders of his horse. The hardcase's eyes gaped open with panic when his handgun clicked on an empty chamber. Death came a split-second later as a slug punched a hole in his heart. Swinging his horse around the corner of the hotel, Chase reined up hard when he spotted Traxel heading out after two horsemen heading toward the river.

He swung his lamed horse around and back to Main Street and dropped to the ground. Quickly he claimed the hardcase's horse, a big, ugly hammerhead, and found the street just vacated by Matt Traxel and the other horsemen.

"Couldn't be sure," he muttered, "but those up front were that damned Scotsman and Raven."

He let the horse have its head until the lane swung north to pass along the river. He couldn't see those he was pursuing, but all Chase had to do was follow the wide splattering hoofmarks. The tracks spun down a crumbling bank, and then he saw a horseman just emerging from the swollen waters then vanishing into thick underbrush. Without hesitating, Chase spurred the hammerhead into the swirling waters. Just as the horse found footing on the opposite reaches of the river, a couple of shots rang out, and all Chase could say was "Raven?"

He lashed the reins hard at the hammerhead's shoulders to urge it into the thorny bushes. A muttered curse came from Chase when a branch whiplashed back at his arm wound. The underbrush seemed an endless obstacle of wet stinging branches growing high so he couldn't make out what lay ahead. When he cleared the underbrush, it was to come across low sandy dunes and hills gaped with draws. Somehow he'd gauged those shots had come from his right, and he reined into a long shadow-strewn draw. When the hammerhead whickered, Chase saw a saddled horse just shying away, and sprawled ahead on the soggy ground was the still form of its rider. He rode over and stared down at Ian MacGregor's dead body.

"About the only way you'll separate one of your breed from your blood money."

From here on Chase had little difficulty in picking up the trail left by Matt Traxel and the other rider. Even in daylight the rough terrain kept a man holding his horse to an easy canter. But the long pacing between the tracks of the other horses revealed they were cutting along at a gallop. And they were angling more to the northeast. This surprised Chase, for he figured a man like Matt Traxel would beeline west for the Rockies. Maybe Traxel had gotten to know this country and was heading for some secret hideout.

Later on, but within the hour, Chase came over a rise and on its downward side saw the ground strewed where one of the horses had gone down. He gazed at where the other rider dismounted, and judged from the size of the bootprints it was Traxel. Then he glimpsed a torn piece of buckskin, and Chase swung down and picked it up.

"Raven tore it from her dress. Yes . . . those smaller tracks are hers . . . where she climbed into the saddle again."

As Chase cantered on, it was somewhat hesitantly, not that he feared an ambush so much, but the way this had turned into a lightning storm. The sky seemed to be filled with an acrid smell despite the fact it was raining.

"What a minute. I know this place. Back a spell this is where those Apache scouts caught up with me."

He let his gaze go far ahead to the varying hills and rises, and then he knew what it was that had tightened the skin on his face, why he was reminded of those Apache scouts. He came through a copse of firs to lay eyes on unrelenting bolts of lightning jagging out of the stormy sky at the place that had almost claimed him.

"The . . . hogback. . . ."

Without thinking he brought the hammerhead into a run, knowing that if Matt Traxel intended making his way up that terrible hill he would probably die as would Raven. Then he saw movement along a draw, a short distance ahead. Matt Traxel must have spotted his pursuer at the same time, for he brought his horse ahead at a gallop while grasping the reins of the other horse. Both horses passed out of Chase's range of vision for a moment as

Chase swept down into the draw.

He came out of it and brought the hammerhead almost to the base of the hogback. At first he couldn't see them, but moments later they came out from behind a jumbling of boulders in their upward climb. Accompanying them at every strained lifting of hoofs and clear across the broad reach of hill were bolts of lightning. Now Chase had no choice but to venture upon a place where he'd cheated death once before.

"Move it!" he urged the hammerhead.

Without warning, and as Matt Traxel saw through flinching eyes that he was almost nearing the crest, a terrible flash of light struck down to chip away stony splinters from a boulder. The knify edges of those splinters tore into his face to blind him, forcing him to release his grasp on the reins belonging to Raven's horse. Though her boots had been lashed to the stirrups, with another rope snugged around her wrists, Raven managed to swing her horse around and let it go plunging recklessly down the hogback.

"No, damn you!" raged the gunfighter. Disregarding his bleeding face, and the lightning, he unleathered his handgun and brought it to bear on Raven Donavan. His first shot missed to punch away from a boulder.

Down below, Chase saw all of this as he pulled out his own handgun. As his finger tightened on the trigger, the man above and his horse seemed to be haloed by a frightening ball of fire. One moment there was a man seated on a bronc, the next Matt Traxel seemed to have just disappeared, but in the

221

harsh glare of lightning Chase couldn't be certain what had just happened.

"Raven!" he shouted.

All he could do was tell her of his presence as Raven clung to her horse sliding now on its belly, finally to slam into mesquite clumps.

As he rode up toward her, the woman he loved called out, "Don't come up . . . the lightning. . . ."

At last when Chase was close enough, he dropped out of the saddle and wormed his way around the mesquite. One glance told him the horse was dying, but he saw the danger to Raven in the way it was still struggling and thrashing about with its forelegs. He pulled out his knife and cut the ropes tying her boots to the stirrups, and then she was in his arms and Chase was carrying her down toward his standing horse. Only when they were off the hogback and he'd found a small cave to shield them from the weather did he free her wrists.

"They hit Jacob's place yesterday . . . our place before that." Something wrenched at his body when tears began spilling out of Raven's eyes, and then he realized she knew her son was dead. "It's . . . all my fault—"

All Raven could do at that moment was just stare at her husband. Still framed deep in her mind was the sight of Matt Traxel killing her son. Was this all that life was about . . . being faced with the death of those she loved . . . keeping on living just to face more men like Traxel. But through her grief Raven saw how what had happened was tearing Chase Donavan apart.

"This is what I have to say, my husband." She

222

took his hand in hers. "Despite what has happened . . . you are my heart . . . my life."

"As you are mine. But enough of this place. We'll head out for Oregon or California."

"That means these men have won."

"Raven, I've simply had enough of . . . of fighting men like Traxel and my past. And Jesse. . . ."

"We will bury our son. But we will not leave our home along the Purgatoire."

"All that's left of our homestead is ashes."

"The men who brought me here were carrying gold in their saddlebags. It is up there now."

"Money that's bloodstained. It seems to be letting up. Once this lightning stops I'll see what's left up there. Maybe some of the money is ours. Enough, anyway, to help us rebuild . . . if that's what you truly want."

"Back in Oklahoma I was considered to be just a piece of property, something to be bartered for and used. And you, Chase, these many years you've been fleeing from your past. I think it is time to take a stand, my love."

He gathered Raven in his arms and held her there until there appeared overhead a speck of blue sky through the sullen clouds. Dropping away at that moment was a lot of Chase Donavan's weariness while bits and pieces from his past seemed to shred away, for he realized through a grateful smile that what he held in his arms was his future.

"Sodbusting's a hard lifestyle."

"Well?"

"Guess I can weather that too."

THRILLERS BY WILLIAM W. JOHNSTONE

THE DEVIL'S CAT   (2091, $3.95)
The town was alive with all kinds of cats. Black, white, fat,
scrawny. They lived in the streets, in backyards, in the
swamps of Becancour. Sam, Nydia, and Little Sam had
never seen so many cats. The cats' eyes were glowing slits as
they watched the newcomers. The town was ripe with evil.
It seemed to waft in from the swamps with the hot, fetid
breeze and breed in the minds of Becancour's citizens.
Soon Sam, Nydia, and Little Sam would battle the forces
of darkness. Standing alone against the ultimate preda-
tor — The Devil's Cat.

THE DEVIL'S HEART   (2110, $3.95)
Now it was summer again in Whitfield. The town was
peaceful, quiet, and unprepared for the atrocities to come.
Eternal life, everlasting youth, an orgy that would span
time — that was what the Lord of Darkness was promising
the coven members in return for their pledge of love. The
few who had fought against his hideous powers before, be-
lieved it could never happen again. Then the hot wind began to blow — as black as evil as The Devil's Heart.

THE DEVIL'S TOUCH   (2111, $3.95)
Once the carnage begins, there's no time for anything but
terror. Hollow-eyed, hungry corpses rise from unearthly
tombs to gorge themselves on living flesh and spawn a new
generation of restless Undead. The demons of Hell cavort
with Satan's unholy disciples in blood-soaked rituals and
fevered orgies. The Balons have faced the red, glowing eyes
of the Master before, and they know what must be done.
But there can be no salvation for those marked by The
Devil's Touch.